John Geddie

The Balladists

Famous Scots Series

John Geddie

The Balladists
Famous Scots Series

ISBN/EAN: 9783744766401

Printed in Europe, USA, Canada, Australia, Japan

Cover: Foto ©Andreas Hilbeck / pixelio.de

More available books at **www.hansebooks.com**

THE BAL: LADISTS

BY JOHN : : : GEDDIE

FAMOUS SCOTS: SERIES

PUBLISHED BY
OLIPHANT ANDERSON
& FERRIER·EDINBVRGH
AND LONDON

The designs and ornaments of this volume are by Mr. Joseph Brown, and the printing from the press of Messrs. T. and A. Constable, Edinburgh.

PREFACE

NOT much more has been attempted in these pages than to extract the marrow of the Scottish Ballad Minstrelsy. They will have served their purpose if they help to awaken, or to renew, a relish for the contents of the Ballad Book. To know and love these grand old songs is its own exceeding great reward; and it is also, alas! almost the only means now left to us of knowing something concerning their nameless writers.

Questions involving literary or critical controversy as to the age and genuineness of the ballads have been, as far as possible, avoided in this popular presentation of their beauties and their qualities; and in case any challenge may be made of the origin or authenticity of the passages quoted, I may say that, in nearly every case, I have prudently, and of purpose, refrained from giving the authority for my text, and have taken that which best pleases my own ear or has clung most closely to my memory.   J. G.

July 1896.

CONTENTS

CHAPTER I

BALLAD CHARACTERISTICS

' Layés that in harping
Ben y-found of ferli thing ;
Sum beth of wer, and sum of wo,
Sum of joye and mirthe also ;
And sum of treacherie and gile ;
Of old aventours that fell while ;
And sum of bourdes and ribaudy ;
And many ther beth of faëry,—
Of all things that men seth ;
Maist o' love forsoth they beth.'

The Lay of the Ash.

WHO would set forth to explore the realm of our Ballad Literature needs not to hamper himself with biographical baggage. Whatever misgivings and mis-adventures may beset him in his wayfaring, there is no risk of breaking neck or limb over dates or names. For of dates and names and other solid landmarks there are none to guide us in this misty morning-land of poetry. The balladist is 'a voice and nothing more' —a voice singing in a chorus of others, in which only faintly and uncertainly we sometimes fancy we can make out the note, but rarely anything of the person or history, of the individual singer. In the hierarchy of song, he is a priest after the order of Melchisedec—without father or mother, beginning of days or end of life.

The Scottish ballads we may thus love and know by heart, and concerning their preservation, their collection, their collation, we may gather a large store of facts. But the original ballad-writers themselves must remain for us the Great Unknown. Here and there one can lay down vague lines that seem to confine a particular ballad, or group of ballads, within particular bounds of place and of time. Here and there one seems to get a glimpse of the balladist himself, as onlooker or as actor in the scenes of fateful love and deathless grief which he has fixed for ever in the memory of men of his race and blood. There are passages in which, in the light and heat of battle, or in agony of terror or sorrow, we are made to see something of the minstrel as well as his theme. But by no research are we likely at this late date to recover any clew to the birthplace or to the lineaments of the life and face of the grand old poet who wrote the grand old ballad of *Sir Patrick Spens*; nor do towns contend for the honour of having produced the sweet singer of *Kirkconnel Lea*, the blithe minstrel of *Glenlogie*, or the first of all the bards who made the *Dowie Dens of Yarrow* vocal with the song of unavailing sorrow.

And in truth towns—even such towns as were in those days—could have had but little to do with the birth

and shaping of the Scottish Balladists. Chief among
the marks by which we may the true ballad-maker
know among the verse-makers of his age, is the
open-air feeling that pervades his thought and style.
Like the Black Douglas, he likes better to hear the
laverock sing than the mouse cheep. It is not only
that he cares to tread 'the bent sae brown' rather than
the paved street; that the tragedies of fiery love and
hate quenched by death, in which he delights, are more
often enacted under the blue cope of heaven than
under vault of stone. What we seem to feel is that
these simple old lays, in which lives a passion that
still catches the breath and makes the cheek turn
pale—whose 'words of might' have yet the power to
waft us, mind and sense, into the 'Land of Faëry,'
must have been conceived and brought to full strength
under the light of the sun and the breath of the wind.
'The Muse,' says Robert Burns, himself of the true
kin of the balladists :

> 'The Muse, nae Poet ever fand her,
> Till by himsel' he learned to wander,
> Adown some trottin' burn's meander,
> An' no think lang.'

Certainly no true ballad was ever hammered out at
the desk. It may have been wrought and fashioned
for singing in bower or hall ; but the fire that shaped
it was caught, in gloaming grey or under the 'lee
licht o' the mune,' in birken shaw or by wan
water.

It is true that one of the earliest of the Scots ballad-makers whose names have been handed down to us—Robert Henryson, who taught the Dunfermline bairns in the hornbook in the fifteenth century—has told us that he sought inspiration at the ingleside over a glass :

> 'I mend the fyre, and beikit me about,
>   Then tuik ane drink my spreitis to confort,
> And armit me weill fra the cold thairout ;
>   To cut the winter nicht, and mak it schort,
>   I tuik ane quhair, and left all uther sport.'

But this was while conning, in cold weather, the classic tale of *Troilus and Cressid.* *Robin and Makyne,* which among Henryson's acknowledged pieces (except *The Bluidy Sark*) comes nearest to our conception of the ballad—after all it is but a pastoral—has the scent of the 'grene wode' in summer.

In sooth, the Ballad Poet was neither made nor born ; he grew. The 'wild flowers of literature' is the name that has been bestowed, with some little air of condescension, upon the rich inheritance he has left us. They are the purest and the strongest growth of the genius of the race and of the soil; and though they owe little save injury and mutilation to those who have deliberately sought to prune and trim them to please a later taste, they are as full of vigour and sap to-day as they were in the Ballad Age, when such poetry sprung up naturally and spontaneously. It is probable that not one of the old ballads that have come down to us by oral recitation is the product of a single hand; or of twenty hands. The greater its age, and the greater its popular favour, the greater is the number of individual memories and imaginations through which it has been filtered, taking from each some trace of colour, some flavour of style or character, some improving or modifying touch. The 'personal equation' is, in the ballad, a quantity at once immense and unknown. As in Homer's *Iliad*, the voice we hear is not that of any individual poet, but of an age and of a people—a voice simple, almost monotonous, in its rhythmic rise and fall, but charged with meanings multitudinous and unutterable.

The Scottish ballads are undoubtedly, in their present form, the outcome of a long and strenuous process of selection. In its earlier stages, the ballad was not written down but passed from mouth to mouth. Additions, interpolations, changes infinite must have been made in the course of transmission and repetition. Like a hardy plant, it had the power to spread and send down fresh roots wherever it found favourable soil; and in its new ground it always, as we shall see, took some colour and character from the locality, the time, and the race. Golden lines and verses may have been shed in the passage from place to place and down the centuries. But less of this happened, we may feel sure, than a purging away of the dross. As a rule, what was fittest —what was truest to nature and to human nature— survived and was perpetuated in this evolution of the ballad. When, in the course of its progress, it gathered to itself anything that was precious and worthy of remembrance, then, by the very law of things, this was seized and stored in the memories of the listeners and handed down to future generations.

But this process of purging and refining the ballad, so that it shall become—like the language, the proverbs, the folklore and nursery tales, and the traditional music of a nation—the reflection of the history and character of the race itself, if it is to be genuine, must go on unconsciously. As soon as the ballad is written down—at least as soon as it is fixed in print—the elements of natural growth it possesses are arrested. It is removed from its natural environment and means of healthy subsistence and development; and from a hardy outdoor plant it is in danger of becoming a plant of the closet— a potted thing, watered with printer's ink and trimmed with the editorial shears. Ballads have sprung up and blossomed in a literary age; but as soon as the spirit that is called literary seizes upon them and seeks to mould them to its forms, they begin to droop and to lose their native bloom and wild-wood fragrance. It is because they neglect, or are ignorant of, literary models and conventions, and go back to the 'eternal verities' of human passion and human motive and action— because they speak to 'the great heart of man'—that they are what they are.

Few of our ballads have escaped those sophisticated touches of art, which, happily, are easily detected in the rough homespun of the old lays. Walter Scott, the last of the minstrels, to whom ballad literature owes more than to any who went before or who has come after him, was himself not above mending the strains gathered from the lips of old women, hill shepherds, and the wandering tribe of cadgers and hawkers, so that one is sometimes a little at a loss to tell what is original and what is imitation. But even the Wizard's hand is not cunning enough to patch the new so deftly upon the old that the difference cannot be detected. The genuine ballad touch is incommunicable; to improve upon it is like painting the lilies of the field.

In the ranks of the Balladists, then, we do not include the many writers of merit—some of them of genius—who have worked in the lines of the elder race of singers, copying their measures and seeking to enter into their spirit. The studied simplicity, the deliberate archaisms, the overstrained vigour or pathos of these modern ballads do but convince us that the vein is well-nigh worked out. The writers could not help thinking of their models and materials; the old minstrels sang with no thought but telling what they saw with their eyes and heard with their ears. But even in these days the precious lode of ballad poetry will sometimes break to the surface; a phrase or a whole verse, fashioned in the Iron Age, will recall the Age of Gold. Scott has many such; and, to take a more modern instance, the spirit of *Sir Patrick Spens* seems to inspire almost throughout George Mac Donald's *Yerl o' Watery Deck*, now with a graphic stroke of description, anon with a sudden gleam of humour, as when the Skipper, in haste to escape his pursuers, hacked with his sword at the stout rope that bound his craft to the pier,

> 'And thocht it oure weel made';

and again when the King's Daughter chose between father and lover in words that leap forth like a sword from its scabbard:

> 'I loot me low to my father for grace,
>   Down on my bended knee;
> But I rise, and I look my king in the face,
>   For the Skipper's the king o' me.'

But even here, where we touch high-water mark of the latter-day Scottish ballad, one seems to find a faint reminiscence of stage-setting and effect, of purposed antithesis, of ethical discriminations unfamiliar to the manner and mode of thought of the ancient balladist. The latter, it may be said, does not stop to think or to analyse or moralise; he feels, and is content to tell us in the most direct and naïve language, all that he has felt. He has not learned the new trick of introspection; he is guided by intuition and the primæval instincts. He carries from his own lips to ours a draught of pure, strong, human passion, stirred into action by provocations of love, jealousy, revenge, and grief such as visit but rarely our orderly, workaday modern world. He renders for us the 'form and express feature' of his time, and though the draughts-manship may be rude, it is free from suspicion of either flattery or bias. It is not enlisted in the cause of any moral theory or literary ideal. It is, so far as it goes, truth naked and not ashamed.

But the native-grown ballad takes also colour from the ground whence it springs. It has the tang of the soil as well as the savour of the blood. Fletcher of Saltoun's hackneyed epigram, 'Let me make a country's ballads, and let who will make its laws,' does not embody all the truth. A country and the race inhabit-ing it may not be responsible for the laws that govern it. But a country and a people may rightly be tried and judged by their ballads—their own handiwork; their own offspring. The more cultured and highly-developed products of a national literature, however healthy, however strong and beautiful, must always owe much to neighbouring and to universal influences. Like the language and manners of the educated classes of a nation, they conform more or less to models of world-wide and age-long acceptance among educated men. But in the ballad one goes to the root of national character, to the pith and marrow of national life and history.

What then, thus questioned, do the Scottish ballads teach us of Scotland and the Scots? Surely much to be proud of. They are among the most precious, as they are among the oldest, of our possessions as a people. Nay, it may be held that they are the best and choicest of all the contributions that Scotland has made to poetry and story. They are written in her heart's blood. Even the songs of Burns and the tales of Scott must take second rank after the ballads; their purest inspiration was drawn from those rude old lays. In this field of national literature, at least, we need not fear comparison with any other land and people. Our ballads are distinctly different, and in the opinion of unbiassed literary judges, also distinctly superior to the rich and beautiful ballad-lore of the Southern Kingdom. One can even note an expressive diversity of style and spirit in the ballads originating on the North and on the South margin of the Border line. The latter do not yield in rough vigour and blunt manliness to the ballads grown on the northern slope of Cheviot. *Chevy Chase* may challenge comparison with *The Battle of Otterburn*, and come at least as well out of the contest as the Percy did from his meeting with the Douglas; and in many other ballads which the two nations have in common—*The Heir of Linn*, for example—the English may fairly be held to bear away the bell from the Scottish version. We do not possess a group of ballads pervaded so thoroughly with the freedom and delight of living under 'the leavés greene' as those of the Robin Hood Cycle; although we also have our songs of the 'gay greenwood'; although bows twanged as keenly in Ettrick Forest and in Braidislee Wood as in Sherwood itself, and we can even claim, partly, perhaps, as a relic of the days when the King of Scotland was Prince of

Cumbria and Earl of Huntingdon, the bold Robin and his merry men among the heroes of our ballad literature.

But, on the whole, mirth and light-heartedness are very far from being characteristics of the Scottish ballads. Of ballad themes in general, it has been said that they concern themselves mainly with the tragedy and the pathos of the life of feudal and early times; while, on the other hand, the folk-song reflects the sunnier hours of the days of old. This is peculiarly true of the Scottish ballads. The best of them are dipped in gloom of the grave. They breathe the very soul of 'the old, unhappy far-off times.' Even over the true lovers, Fate stands from the first with a drawn sword; and the story ends with the 'jow of the deid bell' rather than with the wedding chimes. Superstitious terrors, too, add a shadow of their own to these tragedies of crossed and lawless love and swift-following vengeance. In this respect, the Scottish ballads are more nearly akin to the popular poetry of Denmark and other countries across the North Sea, than to that of our neighbours across the Tweed. There are a score of ballads that agree so closely in plot and structure, and even in names and phrases, with Norse or German versions, that it is impossible to doubt that they have been drawn directly from the same source. Either they have been transplanted thither in the many descents which the Northmen made on Scotland, as is witnessed not only by the chronicles, but by existing words, and customs, and place-names scattered thickly around our coasts; or, what may perhaps be as strongly argued, both versions may have come from an older and common original.

Celtic influences are also present, although scarcely, perhaps, so directly manifest as might have been expected, considering that the Celtic race and speech must at one time have been spread almost universally over Scotland; they appear rather in the spirit than in the plot and scene and characters of the typical Scottish ballad. They supply, unquestionably, a large portion of that feeling of mystery, of over-shadowing fate, and melancholy yearning—that air of another world surrounding and infecting the life of the senses—which seems to distinguish the body and soul of Scottish ballad poetry from the more matter-of-fact budget of the English minstrels.

But it has to be remembered that the matrix of the ballads that have taken first place in the love and in the memory of Scotland was the region most remote and isolated from the Highlands and the Highlanders during the ballad-making era. This is the basin of the Tweed—the howms of Yarrow; Leader haughs and Ettrick shaws; the clear streams that flow past ruined abbey and peel-tower, through green folds of the Cheviots and the Lammermuirs, that for hundreds of years were the chosen homes of Border war and romance. Next after these come the banks of Clyde and Forth; Annan Water and the streams of Ayr and

Galloway; and ballads and ballad localities, differing somewhat, in theme and structure, in mood and metre, from those of the South, as Aberdonian differs from Borderer, and the Men of the Mearns from the Men of the Merse, are found scattered thinly or sprinkled thickly over the whole North, by Tay, and Dee, and Spey.

These latter streams are partly without and partly within the Highland Line, across which, as un-acquainted with a language that has its own rich and peculiar store of legend and ballad poetry, we do not propose to penetrate; sufficient field for explora-tion is provided by the Scots ballads in Scots. But when these were in the making, the Highland Line must have run down much lower into the Lowlands than it does to-day; the retreating Gaelic had still out-posts in Buchan, and even in Fife, and Ayr, and Galloway. In the ballads of the North-eastern Counties, the feuds of Highland chiefs and the raids of Highland caterans make themselves seen and felt, too visibly and not too sympathetically, in the ditties of their Lowland neighbours. 'The Hie-landmen' play the part that the English clans from Bewcastle and Redesdale play in the Border ballads. The 'Red Harlaw' in those boreal provinces was a landmark and turning-point in history and poetry, as Bannockburn or Flodden was in the South. By Hangingshaws or Hermitage Castle they knew little of the Highlander, being too much absorbed in their own quarrels; on Donside and in the Lennox they knew him better than they liked him; and it was not until a comparatively recent period of literary history that the kilted warrior began to take his place as a heroic and imposing figure in the poetry and prose of the Scottish vernacular.

Making all allowance for borrowings and influences drawn from without, may we not still say that the Scottish ballad owes nearly all that is best in it—the sweetness not less than the strength of this draught of old poetry and passion—to the land and to the folk that gave it birth? A land thrust further into the gloom and cold of stormy seas than the Southern Kingdom; a land whose spare gifts are but the more esteemed by its children because they are given so grudgingly, whose high and bleak and stern features make the valleys they shelter the more lovely and loved from the contrast; a race whose blood has been blended of many strains, and tempered by long centuries of struggle with nature and with outside enemies; perfervid of spirit and dour of will; holding with strong grip to the things of this world, but never losing consciousness of the nearness and mystery of the world of things invisible; with a border-line on either side of them that for hundreds of years had to be kept with the strong hand and the stout heart, and behind them a background of history more charged with trouble and romance than that of almost any other nation in Europe—where should the ballad draw pith and sap and colour if not on such a soil and among such a people? If Mr. Buckle was able to trace the complexion and form of Scottish religion in the climate and configuration of Scotland, much more easily should we be able to find the atmosphere and scenery of Scotland reflected in her ballads.

CHAPTER II

BALLAD GROWTH AND BALLAD HISTORY

Clown—What hast here ? ballads?
Mopsa—Pray now, buy some : I love a ballad in print, a' life ; for then we are sure they are true.— *Winter's Tale.*

THERE is probably not a verse, there is scarcely a line, in the existing body of Scottish ballad poetry that can be traced with certainty further back than the sixteenth century. Many of them chronicle events that took place in the seventeenth century, and there are a few that deal with even later history. It may seem a bold thing, therefore, to claim for these traditional tales in verse the much more venerable antiquity implied in what has been said in the previous chapter. If we were to be guided by the accessible literary and historical data, or even by the language of the ballads themselves, we should be disposed to believe that the productive period of ballad-making was confined within two or at most three hundred years.

It would be more than rash, however, to imagine that ballads did not live and grow and spread in the obscure but fertile ground of the popular fancy and the popular memory, because they did not crop up in the contem-

24

porary printed literature, and were overlooked by the dry-as-dust chroniclers of the time. Nor is it a paradox to say that a ballad may be older, by ages, than the hero and the deeds that it seems to celebrate. Like thistledown it has the property of floating from place to place, and even from kingdom to kingdom and from epoch to epoch, changing names and circumstances to suit the locality, and attaching itself to outstanding figures and fresh events without changing its essential spirit and character. The more formal Muses despised these rude and unlettered rhymes—when they noticed them at all it was in a disdainful or patronising spirit— and this holds true of the eighteenth century almost as much as of the sixteenth. It is not that ballad poetry was dumb, but that history was deaf and blind to its beauties.

Nor is any adverse judgment as to the antiquity of the Scottish ballad to be drawn from the comparative modernity of the style and language. The presence of archaisms in a ballad that claims to have been handed down by oral repetition from a remote period is, on the contrary, a thing to raise suspicion as to its genuineness. The ballad, as has been said, is a living and growing organism ; or at least it is this until it has been committed to print. However deep into the mould of the past its roots run down, its language and idioms should not be much older than the popular speech of the time when it has been gathered into the collector's budget. It is like a plant that, while remaining the same at the heart and root, is constantly casting the old, and putting out fresh, leaves.

Thus the very words and phrases that were intended to give an antique air to *Hardyknut* stamped it as an imitation ; these clumsy and artificial patches were not the true mosses of age. The ballad of true lineage, partly from its simplicity of thought and structure, partly from being kept in immediate contact with the lips and the hearts of the people, is as readily 'under-standed of the general' to-day as when it was first sung.

It has been noted, for instance, that our ballads pre-serve fewer reminiscences of the time when alliteration shared importance with rhyme or took its place in the metrical system. The bulk of them are supposed to come hither from the early sixteenth century, from the reigns of James IV. and James V. ; and in that period of Scottish literature alliteration not only blossomed but often overran and smothered the court poetry of the day. Alliterative lines and verses appear frequently in the ballads, but always with good taste, often with exquisite effect. What phrases are more familiar, more infused with the magic of the ballad-spirit, than the 'wan water,' the 'bent sae brown,' the 'lee licht o' the mune'? When the knight rides forth to see his true love, he mounts on his 'berry brown steed,' and 'fares o'er dale and down,' until he comes to the castle wa', where the lady sits 'sewing her silken seam.' He kisses her 'cheek and chin,' and she 'kilts her green kirtle,' and follows him ; but not so fast as to outrun fate. In the oldest set of *The Battle of Otterburn*, alliteration asserts itself :

> ' The rae full reckless there sche runnes
> To make the game and glee.'

It is but seldom that the balladist avails himself so freely of the 'artful aid' of this device as in *Johnie o' Braidislee*, the vigorous hunting lay that was a favourite with Carlyle's mother :

> ' Won up, won up, my good grey dogs,
> Won up and be unboun' ;
> For we maun awa' to Bride's braid wood,
> To ding the dun deer doun, doun,
> To ding the dun deer doun.'

The words that have had the best chance of coming down to us intact on the stream of ballad-verse, or with only such marks of attrition and wear as might be caused by time and a rough channel, are those to which the popular mind of a later day has been unable to attach any definite meaning ; for instance, certain names of places and houses, titles and functions, snatches of refrains, phrases reminiscent of otherwise forgotten primæval or mediæval customs and the like. These remain bedded like fossils in the more recent deposits, and form a curious study, for those who have time to enter into it, in the archæology and palæontology of the ballad. *Childe Rowland, Hynde Horn, Kempion,* furnish us with words, drawn from the language of Gothic and Norman chivalry, that must have dropped out of the common speech long before the ballads began to be regularly collected and printed. They

recall the gentleness and courtesy, as well as the courage,
that were supposed to be attributes of the 'most perfect
goodly knight'—attributes in which, sooth to say, the
typical knight of the Scottish ballad is not always a
pattern. *Kempion*—'Kaempe' or Champion Owayne—is
supposed to perpetuate the name of 'Owain-ap-Urien,
King of Reged,' celebrated by Taliessin and the other
early Welsh bards. And this is by no means the only
instance in which ballads appear to have distilled the
spirit and blended names and stories out of both Celtic
and Teutonic legend. Thus *Glasgerion*, which in the
best-known Scottish version has become *Glenkindie*, has
been translated as *Glas-keraint*—Geraint, the Blue
Bard—an Orpheus among the Brythons, whose chief
legendary sites, according to Mr. Skene, Professor Rhys,
and other authorities, are to be sought in Scotland and
its borderlands. The fame of this harper, who, like
Glenkindie, could 'wile the fish from the flood,' came
down to the times of Chaucer and Gavin Douglas, and
was by them passed on; the former mentions him in
his *House of Fame* along with Chiron and Orion,

> 'And other Harpers many one,
> With the Briton, Glasgerion.'

It is not too much to conjecture that it was remembered
also in popular poetry; and these and other classical
writers of the Middle Ages, who despised not the common folk and their ways, no doubt drank deeply of
knowledge and inspiration from the clear and hidden
well of English poetry and romance even then existing

in ballad lore. In fact, it seems as probable that the prose and metrical romances of chivalry have been derived from the folk-songs they resemble, as that the ballads have been borrowed from the romances; perhaps both owe their descent to a common and forgotten ancestor.

Is it too much to believe that in our older ballads we hear the echoes of the voices—it may be the very words—of the old bards, the harpers and the minstrels, who sang in the ears of princes and people as far back as history can carry us? We know, by experience of other lands and races, from Samoa to Sicily, that are still in their earlier or later ballad-age, that the making of ballads is almost as old as the making of war or of love—that it long precedes letters, to say nothing of the printed page. It comes as natural for men to sing of the pangs of passion, or of the joys of victory, as to kiss or to fight. For untold generations the harps twanged in the hall, and the song of battle and the song of sorrow found eager listeners. All the while, the same tales, though perhaps in ruder and simpler guise, met with as warm a welcome in road and field and at country merrymaking. Trouvere and wandering minstrel, glee-man and eke gleemaiden, passed from place to place and from land to land repeating, altering, adapting the old stock of heroic or lovelorn ditties, or inventing new ones. They were a law unto themselves in other matters than metres; and had their own guilds, their own courts, and their own kings. The names of all but a few that chance, more than anything else, has preserved, have perished. But time may have been more tender than we know to their thoughts and words, or to their words and music, where these have been fitly wedded together. It may have saved for us some thrilling image as old as the time of the scalds, some scrap of melody which Ossian or Llywarch Hen but improved and handed on. The law of the conservation of force holds good in the world of poetry as well as in the physical world; and all that is dispersed and forgotten in ancient song is not lost. It is fused into the general stock of the nation's ideas and memories; and the richest and purest relics of it are perhaps to be sought in the Scottish ballads.

The chroniclers who set down, often at inordinate and wearisome length, what was said and done in court or council or monastery did not wholly overlook the 'gospel of green fields' sung by the contemporary minstrels. But their notices are provokingly vague and unsatisfactory; no happy thought ever seems to have occurred to any monkish penman that he might earn more gratitude from posterity by collecting ballad verses than by copying the Legends of the Saints—so little can we guess what will be deemed of value by future ages. But in Scotland, as elsewhere, we have reason to believe that every event that deeply moved the popular mind gave rise to its crop of ballads, either freshly invented or worked up out of the old ballad stock. So sharply were incidents connected with the departure of a

Scottish Princess, daughter of King Alexander III., to be the bride of Eric of Norway, imprinted on people's minds that, according to Motherwell's calculation, the ballad of *Sir Patrick Spens* preserves the very days of the week when the expedition set sail and made the land:

> 'They hoisted their sails on a Mononday morn,
>   Wi' a' the speed they may,
>   And they have landed in Norawa'
>   Upon a Wodensday.'

But this has the fault of proving too much. The last virtue that the ballad can claim is that of accuracy. With every desire to find proof and confirmation in the very calendar of the antiquity of this glorious old rhyme, one is disposed to suspect these dates to be a lucky hit; in fact, no sounder evidence than the correct enumeration of the daughters of George, fourth Earl of Huntly, in the old Aberdeenshire ballad:

> 'The Lord o' Gordon had three daughters,
>   Elizabeth, Margaret, and Jean,'

which has led some Northern commentators to assume that its heroine was that Lady Jane Gordon whom Bothwell wronged and divorced, and who afterwards managed to console herself by marrying an Earl of Sutherland and a Lord Ogilvy of Boyne. The tragedy of the death of 'Alexander our King,' and the un-numbered woes that came in its train, was, as we know, celebrated in rhymes of which some scant salvage has come down to us; and the feats of William Wallace and the victories of the Bruce were rewarded

by the maidens singing and the harpers harping in
their praise.   This we learn from a surer source than
the ballads of the Wallace and Bruce Cycle that have
been preserved, and that are neither the best of their
kind nor of unquestioned authenticity.   Blind Harry
was himself of the ancient guild of the Minstrels, and
gathered his materials at a date when the 'gude Sir
William Wallace' was nearer his day than Prince
Charlie is to our own.   His poem is nothing other than
floating ballads and traditional tales strung into epic
form after the manner in which Pausanias is supposed
to have pieced together the *Iliad*; indeed John Major,
who in his childhood was contemporary with the
Minstrel, tells us that he wrote down these 'native
rhymes' and 'all that passed current among the people
in his day,' and afterwards 'used to recite his tales in
the households of the nobles, and thereby get the food
and clothing that he deserved.'

Then nothing could yield more convincing proof of
the prevalence and popularity of the ballad in Scotland
in the period of Chaucer—and nothing also could be
more tantalising to the ballad-hunter—than Barbour's
remark in his *Brus*, that it is needless for him to
rehearse the tale of Sir John Soulis's victory over the
English on the shores of Esk :

> ' For quha sa likis, thai may heir
> Yong women, quhen they will play
> Sing it emang thame ilka day.'

The 'young women,' and likewise the old—bless them

for it !—have always taken a foremost part in the singing and preservation of our old ballads, and even in
the composing of them. Bannockburn set their quick
brains working and their tongues wagging tunefully, in
praise of their own heroes and in scorn of the English
'loons.' Aytoun quotes from the contemporary *St.
Alban's Chronicle* a stanza of a song, which (says the
old writer) 'the maydens in that countree made on
Kyng Edward ; and in this manere they sang :

> '"Maydens of Englande, sore may ye morne,
> For ye have lost your lemans at Bannocksborne,
> With rombelogh."'

Do not these jottings of grave fourteenth century
churchmen, bred in the cell but having ears open to
the din of the camp and the 'song of the maydens,'
recall the exquisite words in *Twelfth Night*, that sum
up the ballad at its best?

> 'It is old and plain :
> The spinsters and the knitters in the sun,
> And the free maids that weave their thread with bones
> Do use to chaunt it ; it is silly sooth,
> And dallies with the innocence of love
> Like the old age.'

In the long struggle with our 'auld enemies' of
England that followed Bannockburn ; in the quarrels
between nobles and king ; in the feuds of noble with
noble and of laird with laird that continued for nearly
three hundred years, themes and inspirations for the
ballad muse came thick and fast. It was not alone, or
chiefly, kingly doings and great national events that

C

awakened the minstrel's voice and strings. Harpers
and people had their favourite clans and names—a
favour won most readily by those who were free
both with purse and with sword. The Gordons of the
North; and, in the South, Graemes, Scotts, Armstrongs, Douglases, are among the races that figure
most prominently in ballad poetry. The great house
of Douglas, in particular, is in the eyes and lips of
romance and legend more honoured than the Stewarts
themselves. The Douglas is the hero of both the
Scottish and English versions of *Chevy Chase*. Hume
of Godscroft, in his *History of the House of Angus*,
written in 1644, has saved for us several scraps of traditional song celebrating the wrongs or the exploits of the
Douglases, some of which must have originated at least
as early as the second half of the fourteenth century,
and can be identified in ballads that are extant and
sung in the present day. One of them, quoted by
Scott in his *Minstrelsy*, and times out of number since,
unmistakably reveals the singer's sympathies. It is the
verse that commemorates the treacherous slaughter of
William, sixth Earl of Douglas, and his brother in 1440,
by that great enemy of his race, James II., after the
fatal 'black bull's head' had been set before them at the
banquet to which they had been invited by the king:

> 'Edinburgh Castle, towne and toure,
>   God grant thou sink for sinne!
> And that even for the black dinoúr
>   Erl Douglas gat therein.'

Another records with glee the Douglas triumph when,

in 1528, 'The Earl of Argyle had bound him to ride' into the Merse by the Pass of Pease, but was met and discomfited at 'Edgebucklin Brae.' In another, and much earlier fragment, recording how William Douglas the 'Knight of Liddesdale,' was met and slain by his kinsman, the Earl of Douglas, at the spot now known as Williamshope in Ettrick Forest, after the Countess had written letters to the doomed man 'to dissuade him from that hunting,' we may perhaps discover a germ of *Little Musgrave*, or trace situations and phrases that reappear in *The Douglas Tragedy, Gil Morice,* and their variants.

In *Johnie Armstrong o' Gilnockie, The Border Widow,* and *The Sang of the Outlaw Murray,* also—in which we should perhaps see the reflection, in the popular mind of the day, of the efforts of James IV. and James V. to preserve order on the Borders—it is on the side of the freebooter rather than of the king and the law that our sympathies are enlisted. Indeed your balladist, like Allan Breck Stewart, was never a bigoted partisan of the law. There is ample proof in the writings of Sir David Lyndsay and others that in the first half of the sixteenth century a number of the Scottish ballads that have come down to us were already current and in high favour among the people, although they have not reached us in the shape in which they were then sung or recited.

Long before this period, however, and on both sides of the Border, the status of the minstrel or ballad-

maker—for in old times the two went together, or
rather were blent in one, like the words and music—
had suffered sad declension. There was no longer
question of royal harpers or troubadours, as Alfred the
Great and as Richard the Lion Heart had been in their
hour of need; or even of bards and musicians held in
high favour and honour by king and court, like
Taillefer or Blondel. 'King's Minstrels' there were
on both sides of Tweed, as is found from Exchequer
and other records. But we suspect that these were
players and singers of courtly and artificial lays.
True, a poet of such genuine gifts as Dunbar had gone
to London as the 'King's singer,' and had recited
verses at a Lord Mayor's banquet that had tickled the
ears of the worshipful aldermen and livery. But these
could hardly have been the natural and spontaneous
notes of the Muse of Scottish ballad poetry. The
written and printed verse of the period had got overlaid
and smothered by the flowers of ornament. As a
French student of our literature has said, 'The roses
of these poets are splendid, but too full blown; they
have expended all their strength, all their beauty, all
their fragrance; no store of youth is left in them;
they have given it all away.'

As has happened repeatedly in our literary history,
simplicity in art, as a source both of strength and of
beauty, was almost forgotten; or its tradition was
only remembered among the humble and nameless
balladists. The only ones, says M. Jusserand, who

escape the touch of decadence, are 'those unknown
singers, chiefly in the region of the Scottish border,
who derive their inspiration directly from the people';
who leave books alone and 'remodel ballads that will
be remade after them, and come down to us stirring
and touching,' like that ride of the Percy and the
Douglas which, spite of his classic tastes, stirred the
heart of the author of the *Art of Poesy* 'like the sound
of a trumpet.'

Thus, like Antæus, poetry sprang up again, fresh and
strong, at the touch of its native earth; 'although
declining in castles, it still thrilled with youth along
the hedges and copses, in the woods and on the
moors'; banished from court, it found refuge in the
wilderness and sang at poor men's hearths and at rural
fairs, where the King himself, if we may believe tradition, went out in romantic quest of it and of adventure,
clad as a *gaberlunzie man*. In the *Complaynt of Scotland*, published in 1549, we have an enticing picture
of the extent to which ballad lore and ballad music
entered into the lives of the country people on the eve
of the Reformation troubles. At the gatherings of the
shepherds, old tales would be told, with or without
stringed accompaniment—of *Gil Quheskher* and *Sir
Walter, the Bauld Leslye*, pieces now probably lost to
us irrecoverably; of the familiar *Tayl of Yong Tamlane*;
of *Robene Hude* and *Litel Ihone*, whose fame, like that
of the prophecies of Thomas of Ercildoune, had
already been firmly established for a couple of cen-

turies; of the *Red Etin,* whose place in folklore is well
ascertained; and of the *Tayl of the Thre Vierd Systirs,*
in which one can snuff the ingredients of the caldron
in *Macbeth.* There were dances, founded on the same
themes—*Robin Hood, Thom of Lyn,* and *Johnie Erm-
strang;* and between whiles the women sang 'sueit
melodious sangis of natural music of the antiquite,
such as *The Hunting of Cheviot* and *The Red Harlaw.'*
But of all this feast which he spreads in our sight, our
author only lets us taste a morsel—a couple of lines
taken apparently from a lost ballad on the fate of the
Chevalier de la Beauté, rubbed down by the rough
Scottish tongue to 'Bawty,' at Billie Mire in 1517.

The great religious and social upheaval that had
already changed the face of England reached Scotland
in a severer form. There was an escape of the *odium
theologicum* which always and everywhere is fatal to
the tenderer flowers of poetry and romance. Men's
minds were too deeply moved, and their hands too full
to look upon ballads otherwise than askance and with
disfavour. The Wedderburns and other zealous reformers set themselves to match the traditional and
popular airs to 'Gude and Godlie Ballates' of their
own invention. The wandering ballad-singer could no
longer count on a welcome, either in the castles of the
nobles or with the shepherds of the hills. Instead of
getting, like Henry the Minstrel, his deserts in 'food
and clothing,' these were apt to come to him in the
shape of the stocks or the repentance-stool. He had

lost caste and character, from causes for which he was not altogether responsible. An ill name had been given to him; and doubtless he often managed to merit it. His type, as it was found on both sides of the Border, is Autolycus, whom Shakespeare must often have met in the flesh about the 'footpath ways,' and at the rustic merrymakings of Warwickshire. Autolycus, too, has known the court, and has found his wares go out of fashion and favour with the great, and has to be content with cozening the ears and pockets of simple country folk. One cannot help liking the rogue, although he is as nimble with his fingers as with his tongue. He has the true balladist's love for freedom and sunshine and the open country. He will not be tied by rule; according to his moral law,

> 'When we wander here and there
> We then do go most right.'

His memory and his mouth, like his wallet, are full of snatches of ballads; and they cover a multitude of sins.

Though no undoubted Scottish specimen was drawn from this pedlar's pack, we know, from the plays of the Elizabethan dramatists and other evidence, that Border minstrelsy had already raised echoes in London town, before King Jamie went thither with Scotland streaming in his train. During the last troublous half century of Scotland's history as an independent kingdom, the raw material of ballads was being manufactured as actively as at any period of her history, especially on the Borders and in the North. It may be called, indeed, the Moss-trooping Age, and the chief members of the Moss-trooping Cycle date from the latter years of the sixteenth century. *The Raid of the Reidswire* happed in 1575; the expedition of *Jamie Telfer of the Fair Dodhead* is conjecturally set down for 1582; *The Lads of Wamphray* commemorates a Dumfriesshire feud of the year 1593; while the more famous incident sung with immortal fire and vigour in *Kinmont Willie* took place in 1596. To the same period belong the exploits of *Dick of the Cow* (who had made a name for himself in London while Elizabeth was on the throne), Archie of Ca'field, Hobbie Noble, Dickie of Dryhope, the Laird's Jock, John o' the Side, and other 'rank reivers,' whose title to the gallows is summed up in Sir Richard Maitland of Lethington's terse verse on the Liddesdale thieves; and their match in spulzying and fighting was to be found on the other side of the Esk and the Cheviot.

With the Union of the Crowns, Sir Walter Scott half sadly reminds us in *Nigel*, one stream of Scottish romance and song ran dry; the end of the Kingdom became the middle of it; and as his namesake, Scott of Satchells puts it, the noble freebooter was degraded to be a common thief. But even the Reformation and the Union did not wipe out original sin or alter human nature. The kingdoms might have outwardly composed their quarrels; but private feuds remained, and even the Martyrs and the Covenanters had their relapses, and loved and sang and slew under the impulse of earthly

passion. *The Dowie Dens o' Yarrow*—perhaps the
most moving and most famous of the Scottish ballads—
is supposed to have sprung, in its present shape at least,
out of a tragic passage that occurred by that stream of
sorrow so late as 1616.

Away in the North, what we may call the ballad-
yielding age, if it came later and had a less brilliant
flowering time, endured longer. They had a fighting
'Border' there that lasted until the '45. The Gordons,
of their own hand, have furnished a ballad literature as
rich, if not quite so choice, as that of the Douglases
themselves. *Glenlogie* and *Geordie* were of the 'gay
Gordons,' and had the 'sprightly turn' that is held to
be an inheritance of the race. *Edom o' Gordon*—Adam
of Auchindoun—did his ruthless work in 1571. It was
in one of their interminable quarrels, begun on the
farther side of Spey, that, in the year 1592, the *Bonnie
Earl o' Moray* fell so far away as Donibristle, in Fife.
The mystery of the *Burning of Frendraught* took place
in 1630; the tragedy of *Mill o' Tiftie's Annie*—one of
the few dramas in which the balladist is content to take
his characters from humble life—is dated, from the
tombstone in Fyvie churchyard, in the year following,
and is placed in Gordon country, and under the shadow
of the Setons that became Gordons. *The Bonnie
House o' Airlie* treats of one of the incidents of the
Civil War, and, for a wonder, in the true ballad fashion;
and it turns, as the balladists are apt to do, a crooked
and misliking look on the 'gleyed Argyll'; while that

fine Deeside ballad, *The Baron o' Bracklay*, deals with an encounter between Farquharsons and Gordons in the period of the Restoration.

After this, however, we hardly meet with a ballad having the antique ring about it, even on the Highland Line. The fine gold had become dim, or mixed with later clay. The mood and condition of the nation had changed. The 'end of the auld sang' of the Scottish Parliament was the end also of the ballad. There was an outburst of national feeling, expressed in song and music, over the Jacobite risings of last century; Allan Ramsay rose like a star at its beginning, and Burns shone out gloriously towards its close. But the expression was lyrical; and not narrative. The ballad of the old type no longer grew naturally and freshly by edge of copse and shaw. The collector had his eye upon it, and was already collecting, comparing, and classifying —and, what was worse, correcting, restoring, and improving.

CHAPTER III

BALLAD STRUCTURE AND BALLAD STYLE

'Strike on, strike on, Glenkindie,
  O' thy harping do not blinne,
For every stroke goes o'er thy harp,
  It stounds my heart within.'
                    Glenkindie.

THE old ballads were made to be sung; or, at least,
to be chanted.   An inquiry whether the traditional
ballad airs preceded the words, or *vice . versâ,* would
probably lead us to no more certain conclusions than
that of whether the egg came before the fowl or the
fowl before the egg.   Both ballads and ballad airs
have come down to us greatly changed and corrupted;
and probably it is the airs that have suffered most from
neglect and from alteration.   Notation of the simple
and plaintive and sweet old melodies appropriated in
the ears and lips of the people to the words of particular ballads came long after the transcribing of the
words themselves.   There are other elements of per-
plexity and difficulty in ballad music which require an
expert to unravel and explain, and which cannot be
entered into here.   The subject is referred to only
because, in the eyes of the original composers and

singers at least, to dissever the words from the tune
would have seemed like parting soul from body; and
because no right notion can be gathered of the Scottish
ballads without bearing in mind the part which the
ancient airs have taken in framing their structure and
in moulding their style.

Like the ballads themselves, the 'sets' of ballad
airs vary with the localities; and even in the same
district different airs will be found sung to the same
words and different words to the same air. But of
many of the older ballads, at least, it may be affirmed
that, from time immemorial, they have been preserved in
a certain musical setting which has not altered more
in transmission from place to place and from generation to generation than have the ballads themselves,
and which has so wrought itself into the texture and
essence of the tale that it is impossible to think of
them apart. The analogy of the Scottish psalmody
may, perhaps, be used in illustration. In it, also, there
is a 'common measure' that can be fitted at will to the
common metre—in the psalms, as in the ballads, the
alternation of lines of four and three accented syllables.
In the one case, as in the other, there is a certain
family resemblance, in the melody as in the theme, that
to the untrained and unaccustomed ear may convey an
impression of monotony. But to each ballad, as to
each psalm, there belongs a peculiar strain or lilt,
touched, as a rule, with a solemn or piercing pathos,
often cast in the plaintive minor mode, that alone can

bring out the full inner meaning of the words, and that is endeared and hallowed by centuries of association. As easily might we explain why the words and air of the 'Old Hundredth' or the 'Old 124th' belong to each other, as analyse the wedded harmony of the verse and music in *The Broom o' the Cowdenknowes*, or *Barbara Allan*, or *The Bonnie House o' Airlie*.

But not all, and not all the sweetest and the best of our ballad strains, are so firmly fixed in the memory as these; because, for one thing, they have not all enjoyed the same popularity of print. As a rule, and until this popularity comes, it may be taken that the greater the variations in tune and in words the greater the age. The late Dean Christie, of Fochabers, an enthusiastic hunter after 'Traditional Ballad Airs,' of which he found great treasure-trove in out-of-the-way nooks of Buchan, Enzie, and other districts of the north-eastern counties, tells us, from his experience, that 'the differences in the versions of the Romantic Ballads, as sung in the different counties, may be taken as a proof of their antiquity.' He had 'seldom heard two ballad-singers sing a ballad in the same way, either in words or music'; and he holds it 'almost impossible to find the true set of any traditional air, unless the set can be traced genuinely to its composer,' a task, it need hardly be said, still more difficult than that of tracing the ballad words to the original balladist. It is also the opinion of this authority, that it is well-nigh impossible 'to arrange the traditional melodies without hearing

them sung to the words of the ballad, the words and
the air being so interwoven.'   May it not be said, with
equal truth, that those who know only the words of
Binnorie, or *Chil' Ether*, or *The Twa Corbies*, and have
never heard the strains, sweet and sad and weird, like
the wind crooning at night round a ruined tower, to
which it has been sung for untold generations, have not
yet penetrated to the inmost soul of the ballad, or got a
grasp of its formative principle?

The refrain is a venerable and characteristic feature
of the ballad and ballad melody.   In its refrains, as in
everything else, Scottish ballad poetry has been peculiarly happy.   Some will have it that they are of much
older date than the ballads themselves.   It has been
suggested that many of them—and these the refrains
that have lost, if they ever possessed, any definite or
intelligible meaning to the ear—may be relics not merely
of ancient song, but of ancient rites and incantations,
and of a forgotten speech.   Attempts have been made
to interpret, for instance, the familiar 'Down, down,
derry down,' as a Celtic invocation to assemble at the
hill of sacrifice—a survival of pagan times when the
altars smoked with human victims.   It need only be
said that these ingenious theorists have not yet proved
their case; and that the origin of the refrain is a subject
involved in still greater obscurity than that of the ballad
itself.

Like the ballad verses and the ballad airs, also, these
'owerwords' are exceedingly variable, and are often

interchangeable. Some of them are 'owerwords' literally; that is to say, they simply repeat or echo a word or phrase of the stanza to which they are attached. A specimen is the verse from *Johnie o' Braidislee*, quoted in the previous chapter. Others, and these, as has been said, among the refrains of most ancient and honourable lineage, bear the appearance of words whose meaning has been forgotten. 'With rombelogh' has come rumbling down to us from the days of Bannockburn; and may even then have been of such eld that the key to its interpretation had already been lost. The 'Hey, nien-nanny' of the Scottish ballad was, under slightly different forms, old and quaint in Shakespeare's time, and in Chaucer's. Still others have the effect upon us of the rhyming prattle invented by children at play. They are cries, naïve or wild, from the age of innocence—cries extracted from the children of nature by the beauty of the world or the sharp and relentless stroke of fate. Of such are 'The broom, the bonnie, bonnie broom,' 'Hey wi' the rose and the lindie o',' 'Blaw, blaw, ye cauld winds blaw,' and their congeners. These sweet and idyllic notes are often interposed in some of the very grimmest of our ballads. They suggest a harping interlude between lines that, without this relief, would be weighted with an intolerable load of horror or sorrow. There are refrain lines—'Bonnie St. Johnston stands fair upon Tay' is an example—which seem to hint that they may have been borrowed from some old ballad that, except for this preluding or interjected note, has utterly 'sunk dumb.' But more noticeable are those haunting burdens which, in certain moods, seem somehow to have absorbed more of the story than the ballad lines they accompany—that appeal to an inner sense with a directness and poignancy beyond the power of words to which we attach a coherent meaning. How deeply the sense of dread, of approaching tragedy, as well as that of colour and locality, is stimulated by the iteration of the drear owerword, 'All alone and alonie,' or 'Binnórie, O Binnórie!' How the horror of a monstrous crime creeps nearer with each repetition of the cry, ' Mither, Mither!' in the wild dialogue between mother and son in *Edward*! Like Glenkindie's harping, every stroke 'stounds the heart within'—we scarce can tell how or why.

Like the early Christians, the old balladists seem to have believed in community of goods. They had a kind of joint-stock of ideas, epithets, images; and freely borrowed and exchanged among themselves not merely refrains and single lines, but whole verses, passages, and situations. Always frugal in the employment of ornament in his text, the balladist never troubled to invent when he found a descriptive phrase or figure made and lying ready to his hand. Plagiarism from his brother bards was a thing that troubled him no more than repeating himself. He lived and sang in times before the literary conscience had been awakened or the literary canon had been laid down—or at least in

places and among company where the fear of these, and
of the critic, had never penetrated; and he borrowed,
copied, adapted, without any sense of shame or remorse,
because without any sense of sin. He has his conventional manner of opening, and his established formula
for closing his tale. In portraiture, in scenery, in
costume, he is simplicity itself. The heroine of the
ballad, and, for that matter, the hero also, as a rule,
must have 'yellow hair.' If she is not a Lady Maisry,
it is a wonder if she be not a May Margaret or a Fair
Annie, although there is also a goodly sprinkling of
Janets, and Helens, and Marjories, and Barbaras in the
enchanted land of ballad poetry. Sweet William has
always been the favourite choice of the balladist, among
the Christian names of the knightly wooers. Destiny
presides over their first meeting. The king's daughters

> 'Cast kevils them amang,
>   To see who will to greenwood gang';

and the lot falls upon the youngest and fairest—the
youngest is always the fairest and most beloved in the
ballad. The note of a bugle horn, and the pair see
each other, and are made blessed and undone. Like
Celia and Oliver in the Forest of Arden they no sooner
look than they sigh; they no sooner sigh than they ask
the reason; and as soon as they know the reason they
apply the remedy. Or, mounted on 'high horseback,'
the lover comes suddenly upon the lady among her
sisters or her bower-maidens 'playin' at the ba'.'

D

> 'There were three ladies played at the ba',
>   Hey wi' the rose and the lindie O !
> There cam' a knight and played o'er them a',
>   Where the primrose blooms so sweetly.
>
> The knight he looted to a' the three,
>   Hey wi' the rose and the lindie O !
> But to the youngest he bowed the knee
>   Where the primrose blooms so sweetly.'

He sends messages that reach his true love's ear, through the guard of 'bauld barons' and 'proud porters,' by his little footpage, who,

> 'When he came to broken brig,
>   He bent his bow and swam,
> And when he came to grass growin',
>   Set down his feet and ran.
>
> And when he came to the porter's yett,
>   Stayed neither to chap or ca',
> But set his bent bow to his breast,
>   And lightly lap the wa'.'

Or the knight comes himself to the bower door at witching and untimely hours—at 'the to-fa' o' the nicht,' or at the crowing of the 'red red cock'—and 'tirles at the pin.' But always treachery, in the shape of envious step-dame, angry brother, or false squire, is watching and listening. Six perils may go past, but the seventh is sure to strike its mark. Even should the course of true love run smoothly almost to the church door, something is sure to happen. Love is hot and swift as flame in the ballads, although it does not waste itself in honeyed phrases. It is quick to take offence ; and at a hasty word the lovers start apart,

> ' Lord Thomas spoke a word in jest,
>   Fair Annet took it ill.'

But more often the bolt comes out of the blue from another and jealous hand. The bride sets out richly apparelled and caparisoned to the tryst with the bridegroom. Her girdle is of gold and her skirts of the cramoisie. Four-and-twenty comely knights ride at her side, and four-and-twenty fair maidens in her train. The very hoofs of her steed are 'shod in front with the yellow gold and wi' siller shod behind.' To every teat of his mane is hung a silver bell, and,

> ' At every tift o' the norland win'
>   They tinkle ane by ane.'

If the voyage is by sea,

> ' The masts are a' o' the beaten gold
>   And the sails o' the taffetie.'

The old minstrel loved to linger over and repeat these details, and his audience, we may feel sure, never tired of hearing them. But they knew that calamity was coming, and would overtake bride and groom before they had gone, by sea or land,

> ' A league, a league,
>   A league, but barely three.'

It might be in the shape of storm or flood. One ballad opens :

> ' Annan Water's runnin' deep,
>   And my love Annie's wondrous bonnie,'

and afar off we see what is going to happen. But greater danger than from salt sea wave or ' frush saugh

bush' is to be apprehended from the poisoned cup of
the slighted rival or the dagger of the jealous brother.
The knight had perhaps forgotten when he came
courting his love to 'spier at her brither John'; and
when she stoops from horseback to kiss this sinister
kinsman at parting, he thrusts his sword into her heart.
The rosy face of the bride is wan, and her white bodice
is full of blood when the gay bridegroom greets her, and
he is left 'tearing his yellow hair.' More often, death
itself does not sunder these lovers dear :

> 'Lady Margaret was dead lang e'er midnicht,
> And Lord William lang e'er day.'

And when they are buried, there springs up from their
graves, as has happened in all the ballad lore and
märchen of all the Aryan nations :

> 'Out of the one a bonnie rose bush,
> And out o' the other a brier,'

that 'met and pleat' in a true lovers' knot in emblem of
the immortality of love, as love was in the olden time.

These are all hackneyed phrases and incidents of the
old balladists, the merest counters, borrowed, worn, and
passed on through bards innumerable. But what fire
and colour, what strength and pathos, continue to live
in them! They smell of 'Flora and the fresh-delved
earth'; they are redolent of the spring-time of human
passion and thought. For the most part they belong
to all ballad poetry, and not to the Scottish ballads
alone. But there are other touches that seem to be

peculiar to the genius of our own land and our own
ballad literature; and, as has been said, one can with
no great difficulty note the characteristic marks of the
song of a particular district and even of an individual
singer. The romantic ballads of the North, for example,
although in no way behind those of the Border in
strength and in tenderness, are commonly of rougher
texture. They lack often the grace which, in the versions sung in the South, the minstrel knew how to
combine with the manly vigour of his song; they are
content with assonance where the other must have
rhyme; and in many long and popular ballads, such as
Tiftie's Annie and *Geordie*, there is scarcely so much as
a good sound rhyme from beginning to end. One
sometimes fancies that these Aberdonian ballads bear
signs of being 'nirled' and toughened by the stress of
the East Wind; they are true products of a keen, sharp
climate working upon a deep and rich, but somewhat
dour and stiff, historic soil.

Whether they come from the north or the south side
of Tay, whether they use up the traditional plots and
phrases, or strike out an original line in the story and
language, our ballads have all this precious quality, that
they reflect transparently the manners and morals of their
time, and human nature in all times. Their vast superiority, alike in truth and in beauty, over those imitations
of them that were put forward last century as improve-
ments upon the rude old lays, may best be seen, perhaps, by laying the old and the new 'set' of *Sir James*

the Rose side by side, or comparing verse by verse
David Mallet's much vaunted *William and Margaret,*
with the beautiful old ballad, *There came a ghost to.*
Marg'ret's door.   There is indeed no comparison.
The changes made are nearly all either tinsel ornaments or mutilations of the traditional text, which an
eighteenth century poetaster had sought to dress up to
please the modish taste of the period.   Nothing can be
more out of key with the simple, direct, and graphic
style of the Scottish ballads, dealing with elemental
emotions and the situations arising therefrom, than a
style founded on that of Pope, unless it be the style of
the modern poet and romancist of the analytical and
introspective school.

  If there ever be matter of offence in the traditional
ballad, it resides in the theme and not in the handling
and language.   Whatever be its faults, it never has
the taint of the vulgar; it avoids the suggestive with
the same instinct with which it avoids the vapid adjec-
tive; it is the antithesis of the modern music-hall ditty.
The balladist and his men and women speak straight
to the point, and call a spade a spade.

> ‘Ye lee, ye lee, ye leear loud,
>   Sae loud ’s I hear ye lee,’

and

> ‘ O wae betide you, ill woman,
>   And an ill death may ye dee,’

are among the familiar courtesies of colloquy.   In the
telling of his tale, the minstrel puts off no time in

preluding or introductory passages. In a single verse
or couplet he has dashed into the middle of his theme,
and his characters are already in dramatic parley,
exchanging words like sword-thrusts. Take the opening of the immortal *Dowie Dens of Yarrow*, where
the place, time, circumstances, and actors in the fatal
quarrel are put swiftly before us in four lines :

> ' Late at e'en, drinking the wine,
>   And e'er they paid the lawin',
> They set a combat them between,
>   To fight it e'er the dawin'.'

Or still better example, the not less famous :

> ' The king sits in Dunfermline tower,
>   Drinking the blood-red wine.
> Oh, where shall I find a skeely skipper
>   To sail this ship o' mine.'

Or of *Sir James the Rose* :

> ' O, hae ye nae heard o' Sir James the Rose,
>   The young laird o' Balleichan,
> How he has slain a gallant squire
>   Whose friends are out to take him ! '

Or in yet briefer space the whole materials of
tragedy are given to us, as in that widely-known and
multiform legend of the *Twa Sisters* which Tennyson
took as the basis of his *We were two daughters of one
race* :

> ' He courted the eldest wi' glove and wi' ring,
>   Binnorie, O Binnorie !
> But he loved the youngest aboon a' thing,
>   By the bonnie mill dams o' Binnorie.'

Sometimes a brilliant or glowing picture is called up before our eyes by a stroke or two; as—

or

> 'The boy stared wild like a grey goshawk,'

> 'The mantle that fair Annie wore
> It skinkled in the sun ';

or

> 'And in at her bower window
> The moon shone like a gleed ';

or

> 'O'er his white banes when they are bare
> The wind shall sigh for evermair.'

Or, to rise to the height of pity, despair, and terror to which the ballad strains of Scotland have reached, what master of modern realism has surpassed in trenchant and uncompromising power the passages in *Clerk Saunders?*—

> 'Then he drew forth his bright long brand,
> And slait it on the strae,
> And through Clerk Saunders' body
> He's gart cauld iron gae ';

and,

> 'She looked between her and the wa',
> And dull and drumly were his een.'

Has it ever happened, since the harp of Orpheus drew iron tears down Pluto's cheek, that ruth has taken so grim a form as that of *Edom o' Gordon*, as he turned over with his spear the body of his victim?

> 'O gin her breast was white ;
> " I might have spared that bonnie face
> To be some man's delight." '

Is there in the many pages of romance a climax so surprising, so overwhelming—a revelation that in its succinct and despairing candour goes so straight to the quick of human feeling—as that in the ballad of *Gil Morice*?—

> ' " I ance was as fu' o' Gil Morice
> As the hip is wi' the stane." '

To the fountainhead of our ballad-lore the great poets and romancists, from Chaucer to Shakespeare, and from Shakespeare to Wordsworth and Swinburne, and from Gavin Douglas to Burns and Scott and Stevenson, have gone for refreshment and new inspiration, when the world was weary and tame and sunk in the thraldom of the vulgar, the formal, and the commonplace; and never without receiving their rich reward and testifying their gratitude by fresh gifts of song and story, fresh harpings on the old lyre that moved the hearts of men to tears and laughter long before they knew of printed books. The old wellspring of music and poetry is still open to all, and has lost none of the old power of thrilling and enthralling; and the present is a time when a long and deep draught from the Scottish ballads seems specially required for the healing of a sick literature.

CHAPTER IV

THE MYTHOLOGICAL BALLAD

'Oh see ye not that bonnie road
    That winds about yon fernie brae?
Oh that's the road to fair Elfland
    Where you and I this day maun gae.'
                    Thomas the Rhymer.

No scheme of ballad classification can be at all points
complete and satisfactory. We have seen that it is
impossible to classify the Scottish ballads according to
authorship, since authors, known and proved, there are
none. Scarce more practicable is it to arrange them
in any regular order of chronology or locality; and
even when we seek to group them with regard to type
and subject, difficulties start up at every step. A con-
venient and intelligible division would seem to be one
that recognised the ballads as Mythological, Romantic,
or Historical, this last class including the lays of the
foray and the chase, that cannot be assigned to any
particular date—that cannot, indeed, be proved to
have any historical basis at all—but can yet, with more
or less of probability, be assigned to some historical
or *quasi*-historical character. Besides these, there are
groups of ballads that cannot be wholly overlooked—

ballads in which, contrary to the prevailing spirit of this kind of poetry, Humour asserts itself as an essential element; ballads of the Sea; and Peasant ballads, of which, perhaps, England yields happier examples than Scotland—simple rustic ditties, hawked about in broad-sheets, and dating, many of them, no earlier than the present century, that seldom rise much above the doggerel and commonplace, and do not, as a rule, concern themselves with the high personages and high-strung passions of the ballad of Old Romance.

No well-defined frontier can be laid down between the three chief departments of ballad minstrelsy. The pieces in which fairy-lore and ancient superstition have a prominent place—the ballads of Myth and Marvel—have all of them a strong romantic colouring; and the like may be said of the traditional songs of war and of raiding and hunting, as well as of those whose theme is the passion and tragedy of love. Romance, indeed, is the animating soul of the body of Scottish ballad poetry; the note that gives it unity and distinguishes it from mere versified history and folklore. There are few ballads on which some shadow out of the World Invisible is not cast; few where ill-happed love is not a master-string of the minstrel's harp; few into which there does not come strife and the flash of cold steel. Natheless, a broad division into ballads Supernatural, Romantic, and Martial has reason as well as convenience to recommend it; and in a loose and general way such an arrangement should also indicate the comparative age, not indeed of the ballad versions as we know them, but of the ideas and materials of which they are composed.

First, then, of the ballads that are steeped in the element of the supernatural, let it be remembered that it is well-nigh impossible for us in these days, when we have cleared about us a little island of light in the darkness, to understand the atmosphere of mystery that pressed close around the life of man in the age when the ballad had its birth. The Unknown and the Unseen surrounded him on every side. He could scarcely put forth a hand without touching things that were not of this world; and in proportion to the ignorance was the fear. Through the long twilight in which the primæval beliefs and superstitions grew up and became embodied in legend and custom, in *märchen* and ballad, and all through the Middle Ages, man's pilgrimage on earth was indeed through a Valley of the Shadow. It was a narrow way, between 'the Ditch and the Quag, and past the very mouth of the Pit,' full of frightful sights and dreadful noises, of hobgoblins, and dragons, and chimeras dire. Tales that have ceased to frighten the nursery, that we listen to with a smile or at most with a pleasant stirring of the blood and titillation of the nerves, once on a time were the terror of grown men. The ogres and dragons of old are dead, and the Folklorist and the Comparative Mythologist make free of their caves, and are busy setting up, comparing, classifying, and labelling their skeletons for the instruc-

tion of an age of science. But there was a time when
the wisest believed in their existence as an article of
faith, and when the boldest shuddered to hear them
named. What are now idle fancies were once the
most portentous of realities; and in this lies the secret
of the almost universal diffusion of certain typical tales,
beliefs, and observances, and of the fascination which
they have not ceased to exercise over the imagination
of mankind.

Into the subject of the origins, the relationships, and
the signification of these venerable traditions and superstitions of the race and of all races, there is neither
time nor occasion for entering. This oldest and yet
last found of the realms of science is as yet only in
course of being surveyed, and from day to day fresh
discoveries are announced by the eager explorers of
the darkling provinces of myth and folktale. But this
at least may be said, that not in the wide domain of
popular saga and poetry can there be reaped a
richer or more varied harvest of weird and wild and
beautiful fancies, touched by the light that 'never was
on sea or land,' than is to be found in the Scottish
ballads.

From among them one could gather out a whole
menagerie of the 'selcouth' beasts and birds and
creeping things that have been banished from solid
earth into the limbo of Faëry and Romance. They
furnish examples of nearly all the root-ideas and
typical tales which folklorists have discovered in the

vast jungle of popular legends and superstitions—the Supernatural Birth, the Life and Faith Tokens, the Dragon Slayer, the Mermaid and the Despised Sister, Bluebeard of the Many Wives, the Well of Healing, the Magic Mirror, the Enchanted Horn, the Singing Bone, the Babes in the Wood, the Blabbing Popinjay, the Counterpart, the Transformation, the Spell, the Prophecy, the Riddle, the Return from the Grave, the Dead Ride, the Demon Lover, the Captivity in Faëry-land, the Seven Years' Kain to Hell, and a host of others.

Certain of them, like *Thomas the Rhymer* and *Young Tamlane*, are 'fulfilléd all of Faëry.' One can read in them how deeply the old superstition, which some would attribute to a traditional memory of the pre-Aryan inhabitants of Western Europe—to the 'barrow-wights,' pigmies, or Pechts who dwelt in or were driven for shelter to caves and other underground dwellings of the land—had struck its roots in the popular fancy. Probably Mr. Andrew Lang carries us as far as we can go at present in the search for origins and affinities, when he says that the belief in fairies, and in their relatives, the gnomes and brownies, is 'a complex matter, from which tradition, with its memory of earth-dwellers, is not wholly absent, while more is due to a survival of the pre-Christian Hades, and to the belief in local spirits—the Vius of Melanesia, the Nereids of ancient and modern Greece, the Lares of Rome, the fateful Mæræ and Hathors—old imaginings of a world not yet dispeopled of its dreams.' The elfin-folk of the Scottish ballads have some few traits that are local and national; but, on the whole, they conform pretty closely to a type that has now become well marked in the literature as well as in the popular beliefs of European countries. The fairies have been, among the orders of supernatural beings, the pets and favourites of the poets, who have heaped their flowers of fancy above the graves of the departed Little Folk. We suspect that the more graceful and gracious touches in the Fairy Ballad are the renovating work of later hands than the elder balladist; and in the two typical Scottish examples that have been mentioned, it is not difficult to find the mark of Sir Walter.

In the time when fairies still tripped the moonlit sward, they received praise and compliment indeed from the mouths of their human kin, but it was more out of fear than out of love. They were the 'Men of Peace' and the 'Good Neighbours' for a reason not much different from that which caused the Devil's share in the churchyard to be known as the 'Guid Man's Croft,' lest by speaking more frankly of those having power, evil might befall. The tenancy of brake and woodland in the 'witching hours' by this uncanny people was a formidable addition to the terrors of the night:

> ' Up the craggy mountain
> And down the rushy glen,
> We dare not go a-hunting
> For fear of Little Men.

> Wee folk, good folk,
>   Trooping altogether,
> Green jerkin, red cap,
>   And white owl's feather.'

They were tricksy, capricious, peevish, easily offended, malicious if not wholly malevolent, and dangerous alike to trust and to thwart. All this, together with their habit of trooping in procession and dancing under the moon; their practice of snatching away to their underground abodes those who, by kiss or other spell, fall into their hands; and the penance or sacrifice which at every seven years' term they pay to powers still more dread, comes out in the tale of True Thomas's adventure with the Queen of Faëry, and in Fair Janet's ordeal to win back Young Tamlane to earth. Their prodigious strength, so strangely disproportioned to their size, is celebrated in the quaint lines of *The Wee Wee Man*; while from *The Elfin Knight* we learn that woman's wit as well as woman's faith can, on occasion, prove a match for all the spells and riddles of fairyland. The enchanted horn is heard blowing—

> 'A knight stands on yon high, high hill,
>   Blaw, blaw, ye cauld winds blaw!
> He blaws a blast baith loud and shrill,
>   The cauld wind's blawn my plaid awa,'

and, at the spoken wish, the Elfin Knight is at the maiden's side. But the spell the tongue has woven, the tongue can unloose; and the lady brings her unearthly lover first into captivity by setting him a

preliminary task to perform, more baffling than that
'sewing a sark without a seam.'

It is otherwise with True Thomas, as it was with
Merlin before him, and with all the men, wise and
foolish, who have once yielded to the glamourie of
the Elfin Queen and others of her type and sex. The
Rhymer of Ercildoune was probably only a man more
learned and far-seeing than others of his time. His
reputation for Second Sight may rest upon a basis
similar to that which led the mediæval mind to dub
Virgil a magician, and to recognise the wizard in Sir
Michael Scott, the grave ambassador and counsellor of
kings, and, at a later date, enabled the profane vulgar
to discover a baronet of Gordonstoun to be a warlock,
for no better reason than because, with the encourage-
ment of that most indefatigable of ballad collectors,
Samuel Pepys, he gave his attention to the perfecting of
sea-pumps for the royal navy. Whether the Rhymer's
expedition to Fairyland was feigned by the balladist to
explain his soothsaying; or whether, rather, his prophecies were invented as evidence of the perilous gift
he brought back with him from Elfland, research will
never be able to tell us. But the journey True Thomas
made on the fateful day when, lying on Huntlie bank,

'A ferlie he spied wi' his e'e ;
And there he saw a ladye bright
Come riding down by the Eildon Tree,'

was one that many heroes of adventure, before him and
after him, have made in fairy lands forlorn. The scenery

E

and incidents of that strange ride are also among the common possessions of fairy romance. One dimly discerns in them the glimmer of an ancient allegory, of an old cosmogony, that may possibly be derived from . the very infancy of the world, when human thought began to brood over the mysteries of life and time. There are the Broad Path of Wickedness and the Narrow Way of Right, and between them that 'bonnie road' of Fantasy, winding and fern-sown, that leads to 'fair Elfland.' There is a glimpse of the Garden of the Hesperides and its fruits; and a lurid peep into Hades:

> ' It was mirk, mirk nicht and nae starlicht,
>   And they waded through red bluid to the knee;
> For a' the bluid that 's shed on earth
>   Rins through the springs o' that countrie.'

The Palace of Truth as well as of Error is built on fairy ground; and there is a foretaste of Gilbertian humour in the dismay with which the Rhymer hears that he is to be endowed with 'the tongue that can never lie.'

> ' " My tongue is mine ain," True Thomas said;
>   " A goodlie gift you would give me;
> I neither dought to buy or sell
>   At fair or tryst where I may be;
> I dought neither speak to prince or peer
>   Nor ask of grace from fair ladye." ' '

But from his seven years' wanderings in fairyland, that speed like a day upon earth, he wakens up as from a dream, and again he is laid on Huntlie bank, in sight of the cleft Eildon.

Is it not significant that Melrose and Abbotsford, where a later and greater wizard wrought his spells over the valley of the Tweed and Ettrick Forest, should be half-way between the chief scenes of our Fairy Ballads—between the Rhymer's Tower and Carterhaugh? Fair Janet's conduct, when forbidden to come or go by Carterhaugh, where Yarrow holds tryst with Ettrick, lest she might encounter the Young Tamlane, may be traced back to the Garden of Eden, and is of a piece with that of Mother Eve:

> ' Janet has kilted her green kirtle
>   A little abune her knee ;
> And she has braided her yellow hair
>   A little abune her bree ;
> And she 's awa' to Carterhaugh
>   As fast as she could gae.'

There she falls in with the 'elfin grey' who might have been an 'earthly knight'; and he tells her how, as a youth, he had been reft away to fairyland:

> ' There cam' a wind out o' the north,
>   A sharp wind and a snell ;
> A deep sleep cam' over me
>   And from my horse I fell';

as happened to 'Held Harald' and his men in the German legend. But he also tells her how, by waiting at the cross road at midnight on Halloweve, 'when fairy folk do ride,' she may win back the father of her child to mortal shape. That waiting on the dreary heath

while 'a north wind tore the bent,' and what followed,
become the ordeal of Janet's love :

> ' Aboot the dead hour o' the night
>   She heard the bridles ring ;
> And Janet was as glad o' that
>   As any earthly thing.
>
> And first gaed by the black, black steed,
>   And then gaed by the brown,
> But fast she gripped the milk-white steed
>   And pu'ed the rider down ' ;

and holding her lover fast, through all his gruesome
changes of form, she 'borrowed' him from the 'seely
court,' and saved him from becoming the tribute paid
every seven years to the powers that held fairydom in
vassalage.

Another series of transmutations, familiar in ballad and
folklore, is that in which the powers of White and Black
Magic strive for the mastery, generally to the discom-
fiture of the latter, after the manner of the Hunting of
Paupukewis in *Hiawatha*. The baffled magician or
witch—often the mother-in-law or stepmother, the stock
villain of the piece in these old tales—alters her shape
rapidly to living creature or inanimate thing ; but fast as
she changes the avenger also changes, pursues, and at
length destroys. In the ballad of *The Twa Magicians*,
given in Buchan's collection, it is virtue that flees, and
wrong, in the shape of a Smith, of Weyland's mystic
kin, that follows and overcomes.

But, as a rule, the transformations that are made the
subject of the Scottish ballads are of a more lasting

kind; the prince or princess, tempted by a kiss, or at the touch of enchanted wand or ring, is doomed for a time to crawl in the loathly shape of snake or dragon about a tree, or swim the waters as mermaid or other monstrous brood of the seas of romance, until the appointed time when the deliverer comes, and by like magic art, or by the pure force of courage and love, looses the spell. *Kempion* is a type of a class of story that runs, in many variations, through the romances of chivalry, and from these may have been passed down to the ballad-singer, although ruder forms of it are common to nearly all folk-mythology. The hero is one of those kings' sons, who, along with kings' daughters, people the literature of ballad and *märchen*; and he has heard of the 'heavy weird' that has been laid upon a lady to haunt the flood around the Estmere Crags as a 'fiery beast.' He is dared to lean over the cliff and kiss this hideous creature; and at the third kiss she turns into

> 'The loveliest ladye e'er could be.'

The rescuer asks—

> 'O, was it wehrwolf in the wood,
>   Or was it mermaid in the sea?
> Or was it man, or vile womán,
>   My ain true love, that misshapéd thee?'

Nor do we wonder to hear that it was the doing of the wicked and envious stepmother, on whom there straight falls a worse and a well-deserved weird. In

King Henrie, too, it is the stepdame that has wrought the mischief. He is lying 'burd alane' in his hunting hall in the forest, when his grey dogs cringe and whine; the door is burst in, and

> 'A grisly ghost
> Stands stamping on the floor.'

The manners of this *Poltergeist* are in keeping with her rough entrance on the scene; her ogreish appetite is not satisfied even when she had devoured his hounds, his hawks, and his steed. As in the *Wife of Bath's Tale*, and the *Marriage of Sir Gawain* and other legends of the same type, the knight's courtesy withstands every test, and he is rewarded for having given the lady her will:

> 'When day was come and night was gane
> And the sun shone through the ha',
> The fairest ladye that e'er was seen
> Lay between him and the wa'.'

In most cases it is not wise or safe to give entertainment to these wanderers of the night, whether they come in fair shape or in foul. They are apt to prove to be of the race of the *succubi*, from whom a kiss means death or worse. More than one of our Scottish ballads are reminiscent of the beautiful old Breton lay, *The Lord Nann*, so admirably translated by Tom Taylor, wherein the young husband, stricken to the heart by the baleful kiss given to him against his will by a wood-nymph, goes home to die, and his fair young wife follows him fast to the grave. *Alison Gross* is another of those Circes who, by incantation of horn and wand, seek to lower the shape and nature of her lovers to those of the beasts that crawl on their bellies. Sometimes the tempter is of the other sex. Thus *The Demon Lover* is a tale known in several versions in Scotland, and lately brought under notice by Mr. Hall Caine in its Manx form. The frail lady is enticed from her home, and induced to put foot on board the mysterious ship by an appeal, a pathetic echo of which has lingered on in later poetry, and has been quoted as the very dirge of the Lost Cause:

> ' He turned him right and round about,
>   And the tear blindit his e'e ;
> " I would never have trodden on Irish ground
>   If it hadna been for thee." '

They have not sailed far, when his countenance changes, and he grows to a monstrous stature; the foul fiend is revealed. They are bound on a drearier voyage than that of True Thomas—to a Hades of ice and isolation that bespeaks the northern origin of the tale:

> ' "O whaten a mountain's yon," she said,
>   " So dreary wi' frost and snow ? "
> " O yon's the mountain of hell," he cried,
>   " Where you and I must go."

> He strack the tapmast wi' his hand,
>   The foremast wi' his knee ;
> And he brake the gallant ship in twain
>   And sank her in the sea.'

Other spells and charms not a few, for the winning of love and the slaking of revenge, are known to the old

balladists.   We hear of the compelling or sundering
power of the bright red gold and the cold steel.   Lovers
at parting exchange rings, as in *Hynd Horn*, gifted with
the property of revealing death or faithlessness :

> ' When your ring turns pale and wan,
>   Then I 'm in love wi' another man.'

Or, as in *Rose the Red and Lily Flower*, it is a magic
horn, to be blown when in danger, and whose notes
can be heard at any distance.   These are examples of
the 'Life Token' and the 'Faith Token,' known to the
folklore of nearly all peoples who have preserved fragments of their primitive beliefs.   The prophetic power
of dreams is revealed in *The Drowned Lovers*, in *Child
Rowland*, in *Annie of Lochryan*, and in a host of others.
The spells used by witchcraft to arrest birth do not
differ greatly in *Willie's Lady*—the 'nine witch-knots,'
the 'bush of woodbine,' the 'kaims o' care,' and the
'master goat'—from those mentioned in its prototypes
in Scandinavian, Greek, and Eastern ballads and
stories ; and in more than one it is the sage counsels
of 'Billy Blin''—the Brownie—that give the cue by
which the evil charm is unwound.   The Brownie—
the Lubber Fiend—owns a department of legend and
ballad scarcely less important than that possessed by
his relatives, the Elfin folk and the Trolds ; a shy and
clumsy monster, but harmless and good-natured, and
with a turn for hard manual labour that can be turned
to useful account.   Good and ill fortune, in the
ballads, comes often by lot :

'We were sisters, sisters seven,
  Bowing down, bowing down ;
The fairest maidens under heaven ;
  And aye the birks a' bowing.

And we keest kevils us amang,
  Bowing down, bowing down ;
To see who would to greenwood gang,
  And aye the birks a' bowing.'

The birk held a high place in the secret rites and customs of the Ballad Age. It was with 'a wand o' the bonnie birk' that May Margaret went through the mysterious process of restoring her plighted troth to Clerk Saunders ; in other ballads it is done by passes of the hand, or of a crystal rod. When the 'Clerk's Twa Sons o' Owsenford' were brought back to earth by their mother's bitter grief and longing, they wore 'hats made o' the birk' :

'It neither grew in syke or ditch,
  Nor yet in ony sheugh ;
But at the gate of Paradise
  That birk grew green eneuch.'

Birds of the air carry a secret ; there are tongues in trees that syllable men's names ; and even inanimate things cry aloud with the voice of Remorse or of Doom. When the knight wishes to send a message, he speaks in the ear of his 'gay goshawk that can baith speak and flee.' When May Colvin returns home after the fatal meeting at the well, where her seven predecessors in the love of the 'Fause Sir John' had been drowned, the 'wylie parrot' speaks the words that were no doubt ringing in her brain :

'What hae ye made o' the fause Sir John
That ye gaed wi' yestreen?'

And in *Earl Richard* and other ballads, it is the
'popinjay' that proclaims guilt or fear from turret or
tree. One remembers also 'Proud Maisie' walking
early in the wood, and Sweet Robin piping her doom
among the green summer leaves :

'"Tell me, my bonnie bird,
When shall I marry me?"
"When six braw gentlemen
Kirkward shall carry thee"';

and the 'Three Corbies' croaking the most grim and
dismal notes in all the wide, wild range of ballad poetry,
as they feast on the new-slain knight :

'Ye'll sit on his white hause bane,
And I'll pike oot his bonnie blue een ;
Wi' ae lock o' his yellow hair
We'll theak our nest when it is bare.

O mony a ane for him maks mane,
But nae ane kens whaur he is gane,
O'er his white banes when they are bare
The wind shall sigh for evermair.'

But things that have neither sense nor life utter
aloud words of menace and accusation. Lord Barnard's
horn makes the forest echo with the warning notes,
'Away, Musgrave, away!' *Binnorie* embalms the
tradition of the 'singing bone' which pervades the
folklore of the Aryan peoples, and is found also in
China and among the negro tribes of West Africa. A

harper finds the body of the drowned sister, and out of her 'breast-bane' he forms a harp which he strings with her yellow hair. According to a northern version of the ballad, he makes a plectrum from 'a lith of her finger bane.' On this strange instrument the minstrel plays before king and court, and the strings sigh forth :

> 'Wae to my sister, fair Helén !'

In other ballads, the yearning or remorse of the living draw the dead from their graves. In the tale of *The Cruel Mother*, we seem to see the workings of the guilty conscience, which at length 'visualised' the victims of unnatural murder. The bride goes alone to the bonnie greenwood, to bear and to slay her twin children :

> 'She's wrapped her mantle about her head,
>   All alone, and alonie O !
> She's gone to do a fearful deed
>   Down by the greenwood bonnie O !'

The crime and shame are hid ; but peace does not come to her :

> 'The lady looked o'er her high castle wa',
>   All alone and alonie O !
> She saw twa bonnie bairnies play at the ba'
>   Down by yon greenwood bonnie O !

The mother's yearning awakens within her, and she promises them all manner of gifts if they will only be hers. But the voices of the ghost-children rise and pronounce judgment on her :

> ' O cruel mither, when we were thine,
>   All alone and alonie O !
> From us ye did our young lives twine,
>   Doon by yon greenwood bonnie O.'

Elsewhere in these old rhymes may be traced a superstitious belief, which was put in practice as a means of discovering guilt, at least as late as the middle of the seventeenth century—that of the Ordeal by Touch. In *Young Benjie* another test is applied to find the murderer; and at midnight the door of the death-chamber is set ajar, so that the wandering spirit may enter and reanimate for an hour the 'streikit corpse':

> ' About the middle of the night
>   The cocks began to craw;
> And at the dead hour o' the night,
>   The corpse began to thraw.'

It sat up; and with its dead lips told the waiting brethren on whose head justice, tempered with a strange streak of mercy, should fall for the foul slaughter of their 'ae sister':

> ' Ye maunna Benjie head, brothers,
>   Ye maunna Benjie hang,
> But ye maun pyke oot his twa grey een
>   Before ye let him gang.'

In *Proud Lady Margaret*, again, we have a form of the legend, told in many lands, and made familiar, in a milder form, by the classical German ballad of *The Lady of the Kynast*, of a haughty and cruel dame whose riddles are answered and whose heart is at length won

by a stranger knight. She would fain ride home with
him, but he answers her that he is her brother Willie,
come from the other side of death to 'humble her
haughty heart has gart sae mony dee':

> 'The wee worms are my bedfellows
> And cauld clay is my sheets';

and there is no room in his narrow house for other
company. Out of the Dark Country, too, on a similar
errand, on Hallowe'en night, rides the betrayed and
slain knight in *Child Rowland*, the first line of which,
preserved in *King Lear* as it was known in Shakespeare's day, seems to strike a keynote of ballad
romance:

> 'Child Rowland to the dark tower came,'

mumbles the feigned madman in the ear of the poor
wronged king as they tread the waste heath. And the
sequel, as it has come down to us, sustains and
strengthens the spell of the opening:

> 'And he tirled at the pin;
> And wha sae ready as his fause love,
> To rise and let him in.'

The passages that describe the haunted ride in the
moonlight, when the lady has fled from the scene of
her treachery and guilt, are not surpassed in weird
imaginative power, if they are equalled, by anything in
ballad or other literature:

> 'She hadna ridden a mile, a mile,
> Never a mile but ane,
> When she was 'ware o' a tall young man
> Riding slowly o'er the plain.

> She turned her to the right about,
>   And to the left turned she ;
> But aye 'tween her and the wan moonlight
>   That tall knight did she see.'

She set whip and spur to her steed, but 'nae nearer could she get'; she appealed to him, as from a 'saikless,' or guiltless, maid to 'a leal true knight,' to draw his bridle-rein until she can come up with him :

> ' But nothing did that tall knight say,
>   And nothing did he blin ;
> Still slowly rade he on before,
>   And fast she rade behind,'

until he drew rein at a broad river-side.   Then he spoke :

> ' " This water it is deep," he said,
>   " As it is wondrous dun ;
> But it is sic as a saikless maid,
>   And a leal true knight can swim." '

They plunged in together, and the flood bore them down :

> ' " The water is waxing deeper still,
>   Sae does it wax mair wide ;
> And aye the farther we ride on,
>   Farther off is the other side."
>   .   .   .   .   .
> The knight turned slowly round about
>   All in the middle stream,
> He stretched out his hand to that lady,
>   And loudly she did scream.

> " O, this is Hallow-morn," he said,
>   " And it is your bridal day ;
> But sad would be that gay wedding
>   Were bridegroom and bride away.

> But ride on, ride on, proud Margaret,
>   Till the water comes o'er your bree ;
> For the bride maun ride deep and deeper yet
>   Who rides this ford wi' me." '

But the perturbed spirit does not always thus revisit the glimpses of the moon to awaken conscience, to humble pride, or to wreak vengeance.   More often it is the repinings and longings of passionate love that keep it from its rest.   In *märchen* and ballad the ghost of the lover comes to complain that the tears which his betrothed sheds nightly fill his shroud with blood; when she smiles, it is filled with rose leaves. The mother steals from the grave to hap and comfort her orphan children ; their harsh stepmother neglects and ill-treats them, and their exceeding bitter and desolate cry has penetrated beneath the sod, and reached the dead ear.   In. *The Clerk's Sons o' Owsenford*, and in that singular fragment of the same creepy theme, recovered by Scott, *The Wife of Usher's Well*, it is the yearning of the living mother that brings the dead sons back to their home :

> ' " Blaw up the fire, my maidens,
>   Bring water from the well !
> For a' my house shall feast this nicht,
>   Since my three sons are well." '

The *revenants*, silent guests with staring eyes, wait and warm themselves by the fireside, while the ' carline wife' ministers to their wants, and spreads her ' gay mantle ' over them to keep them from the cold, until their time comes :

> ‘ “The cock doth craw, the day doth daw,
>   The channerin' worm doth chide ;
>   Gin we be missed out o' our place
>   A sair pain we must bide.”
>
>   “Lie still, be still a little wee while,
>   Lie still but if we may ;
>   Gin my mother should miss us when she wakes,
>   She 'll gae mad, ere it be day.”
>
>   O it 's they 've taen up their mother's mantle,
>   And they 've hung it on a pin ;
>   “O lang may ye hing, my mother's mantle,
>   Ere ye hap us again.” ’

A chill air as from the charnel-house seems to breathe upon us while reading the lines ; the coldness, the darkness, and the horror of death have never been painted for us with more terrible power than in the ‘Wiertz Gallery’ of the old balladists.

We feel this also in the ballads of the type of *Sweet William and May Margaret*, quoted in Beaumont and Fletcher's *Knight of the Burning Pestle*, where the dead returns to claim back a plighted word ; and at the same time we feel the strength of the perfect love that triumphs over death and casts out fear :

> ‘ “Is there any room at your head, Willie,
>   Or any room at your feet,
>   Or any room at your side, Willie,
>   Wherein that I may creep ?” ’

How miserably the poetical taste of the early part of last century misappreciated the spirit of the ancient ballad, preferring the dross to the fine gold, and tricking out the 'terrific old Scottish tale,' as Sir Walter Scott calls it, in meretricious ornament, may be seen by comparing the original copies with that 'elegant' composition of David Mallet, *William and Margaret*, so praised and popular in its day, in which every change made is a disfigurement of the nature of an outrage. Read the summons of the ghost, still 'naked of ornament and simple':

> ' " O sweet Marg'ret, O dear Marg'ret !
> I pray thee speak to me ;
> Gie me my faith and troth, Marg'ret,
> As I gae it to thee," '

along with the 'improved' version :

> ' "Awake !" she cried, "thy true love calls,
> Come from her midnight grave ;
> Now let thy pity hear the maid
> Thy love refused to save." '

Of a long antiquity most of these Mythological Ballads must be, if not in their actual phraseology, in the dark superstitions they embody and in the pathetic glimpses they afford us of the thoughts and fears and hopes of the men and women of the days of long ago— the days before feudalism ; the days, as some inquisitors of the ballad assure us, when religion was a kind of fetichism or ancestor worship, when the laws were the laws of the tribe or family, and when the cannibal feast may have been among the customs of the race. We cannot find a time when this inheritance of legend was not old ; when it was not sung, and committed to

F

memory, and handed down to later generations in some
rude rhyme. The leading 'types' were in the wallet
of Autolycus; and he describes certain of them with
a seasoning of his grotesque humour, to his simple
country audience. There were the well-attested tale
of the *Usurer's Wife*, a ballad sung, as ballads are
wont, 'to a very doleful tune'—obviously a form of the
Supernatural Birth; and the story, true as it is pitiful,
of the fish that turned to woman, and then back again
to fish, in which he that runs may read an example
from the Mermaid Cycle. They are to be found to-
day, often in debased and barely recognisable guise,
in the hands of the peripatetic ballad-mongers who still
haunt fairs and sing in the streets, and in the memories
of multitudes of country folks who know scarce any
other literature bearing the magic trademark of Old
Romance.

CHAPTER V

THE ROMANTIC BALLAD

'O they rade on, and farther on,
   By the lee licht o' the moon,
Until they cam' to a wan water,
   And there they lichted them doon.'
The Douglas Tragedy.

I⊤ may look like taking a liberty with the chart of
ballad poetry to label as 'romantic' a single province
of this kingdom of Old Romance. It is probably not
even the most ancient of the provinces of balladry,
but it has some claim to be regarded as the central one
in fame and in wealth—the one that yields the purest
and richest ore of poetry. It is that wherein the passion
and frenzy of love is not merely an element or a
prominent motive, but is the controlling spirit and
the absorbing interest.

As has been acknowledged, it is not possible to make
any hard and fast division of the Scottish ballads by
applying to them this or any other test; and mention
has already been made, or account of the mythological
or superstitious features they possess, of a number of the
choicest of these old lays that turn essentially upon
the strength or the weakness, the constancy or the

inconstancy, the rapture or the sorrow of earthly love. Love in the ballads is nearly always masterful, imperious, exacting; nearly always its reward is death and dule, and not life and happiness. But as it spurns all obstacles, it meets its fate unflinchingly. No sacrifices are too great, no penace too dire, no shame or sin too black to turn aside for an instant the rush of this impetuous passion, which runs bare-breasted on the drawn sword.

It is not to the ballads we must go for example— precept of this or of any kind there is none—in the *bourgeois* and respectable virtues; of the sober and chastened behaviour that comes of a prudent fear of consequences, of a cold temperament and a calculating spirit. The good or the ill done by the heroes and heroines of the Romantic Ballad is done on the spur of the moment, on the impulse of hot blood. Whether it be sin or sacrifice, the prompting is not that of con- vention, but of Nature herself. Love and hate, though they may burn and glow like a volcano, are not prodigal of words. It is one of the marks by which we may distinguish the characters in the ballads from those in later and more cultivated fields of literature that, as a rule, they say less rather than more than they mean. They speak daggers; but they are far more apt in using them. At a word or look the lovers are ready to die for each other; but of the language of endearment they are not prodigal; and a phrase of tenderness is sweet in proportion that it is rare.

With the tamer affections it fares no better than with
the moral law when it comes in the path of the master
passion.   Mother and sisters are defied and forsaken ;
father and brethren are resisted at the sword's point
when they cross, as is their wont, the course of true
love.   It is curious to note how little, except as a foil,
the ballad makes of brotherly or sisterly love.   It
finds exquisite expression in the tale of *Chil Ether*
and his twin sister,

> ' Who loved each other tenderly
> 'Boon everything on earth.

> " The ley likesna the simmer shower
> Nor girse the morning dew,
> Better, dear Lady Maisrie,
> Than Chil Ether loves you." '

But for this, among other reasons, the genuine antiquity
of the ballad is under some suspicion.

In modern fiction or drama the lady hesitates between
the opposing forces of love and of family pride and
duty; the old influences in her life do not yield to the
new without a struggle.   But of struggle or indecision
the ballad heroine knows, or at least says, nothing.   A
glance, a whispered word, a note of harp or horn, and
she flings down her ' silken seam,' and whether she be
king's daughter or beggar maid she obeys the spell, and
follows the enchanter to greenwood or to broomy hill,
to the ends of the earth, and to the gates of death.

For when the gallant knight and his 'fair may' ride
away, prying eyes are upon them ; black care and red

vengeance climb up behind them and keep them company. *The Douglas Tragedy* may be selected for its
terseness and dramatic strength, for the romance and
pathos inwoven in the very names and scenes with
which it is associated, as the type of a favourite story
which under various titles—*Earl Brand* and the
Child of Elle among the rest—has, time beyond knowledge, captivated the imagination and drawn the tears
of ballad-lovers. In the best-known Scots version—
that which Sir Walter Scott has recovered for us, and
which bears some touches of his rescuing hand—it is
the lady-mother who gives the alarm that the maiden
has fled under cloud of night with her lover :

> ' Rise up, rise up, my seven bauld sons,
>   And put on your armour so bright,
> And take better care of your youngest sister,
>   For your eldest 's awa' the last night.'

In English variants, it is the sour serving-man or false
bower-woman who gives the alarm and sets the chase
in motion. But there are other differences that enter
into the very essence of the story, and express the
diverse feeling of the Scottish and the English ballad.
In the latter there is a pretty scene of entreaty and
reconciliation ; the lady's tears soften the harsh will of
the father, and stay the lifted blade of the lover, and all
ends merry as a marriage bell. But in the Scottish
ballads fathers and lovers are not given to the melting
mood. In sympathy with the scenery and atmosphere,
the ballad spirit is with us sterner and darker ; and just

as the materials of that tender little idyll of faithful
love, *The Three Ravens*, are in Scottish hands trans-
formed into the drear, wild dirge of *The Twa Corbies*,
the gallant adventure of the *Child of Elle* turns inevit-
ably to tragedy by Douglas Water and Yarrow. But
how much more true to this soul of romance is the
choice of the northern minstrel ! Lady Margaret, as
she holds Lord William's bridle-rein while he deals
those strokes so 'wondrous sair' at her nearest kin, is
a figure that will haunt the 'stream of sorrow' as long
as verse has power to move the hearts of men :

> ' " O choose, O choose, Lady Marg'ret," he cried,
>   " O whether will ye gang or bide?"
> " I 'll gang, I 'll gang, Lord William," she said,
>   " For you 've left me no other guide."
>
> He lifted her on a milk-white steed,
>   And himself on a dapple grey,
> With a buglet horn hung down by his side,
>   And slowly they both rade away.
>
> O they rade on, and farther on,
>   By the lee licht o' the moon,
> Until they cam' to a wan water,
>   And there they lichted them doon.
>
> "Hold up, hold up, Lord William," she said,
>   " For I fear that ye are slain."
> " 'Tis naething but the shadow of my scarlet cloak
>   That shines in the water so plain." '

The man who can listen to these lines without a thrill
is proof against the Ithuriel spear of Romance. He is
not made of penetrable stuff, and need waste no thought
on the Scottish ballads.

To close the tale comes that colophon that as naturally ends the typical ballad as ' Once upon a time '
begins the typical nursery tale :

> ' Lord William was buried in St. Mary's Kirk,
>   Lady Margaret in St. Mary's Quire ;
> And out of her grave there grew a birk,
>   And out of the knight's a brier.
>
> And they twa met and they twa plait,
>   As fain they wad be near ;
> And a' the world might ken right well
>   They were twa lovers dear.'

Birk and brier ; vine and rose ; cypress and orange ;
thorn and olive—the plants in which the buried lovers
of ballad romance live again and intertwine their limbs,
vary with the clime and race ; and just as the ' Black
Douglas ' of the Yarrow ballad—' Wow but he was
rough !'—plucks up the brier, and 'flings it in St. Mary's
Loch,' the King, in the Portuguese folk-song, cuts down
the cypress and orange that perpetuate the loves of
Count Nello and the Infanta, and then grinds his teeth
to see the double stream of blood flow from them and
unite, proving that ' in death they are not divided.'

The scene of the Scottish story is supposed to be
Blackhouse, on the Douglas Burn, a feeder of the
Yarrow, the farm on which Scott's friend, William
Laidlaw, the author of *Lucy's Flittin'*, was born. Seven
stones on the heights above, where the ' Ettrick Shepherd,' with his dog Hector, herded sheep and watched
for the rising of the Queen of Faëry through the mist,
mark the spot where the seven bauld brethren fell.

But Yarrow Vale is strewn with the sites of those tragedies of the far-off years, forgotten by history but remembered in song and tradition. Its green hills enclose the very sanctuary of romantic ballad-lore. Its clear current sings a mournful song of the ' good heart's bluid ' that once stained its wave; of the drowned youth caught in the ' cleaving o' the craig.' The winds that sweep the hillsides and bend ' the birks a' bowing ' seem to whisper still of the wail of the ' winsome marrow,' and to have an undernote of sadness on the brightest day of summer; while with the fall of the red and yellow leaf the very spirit of ' pastoral melancholy ' broods and sleeps in this enchanted valley. St. Mary's Kirk and Loch ; Henderland Tower and the Dow Linn ; Blackhouse and Douglas Craig ; Yarrow Kirk and Deucharswire ; Hangingshaw and Tinnis ; Broadmeadows and Newark ; Bowhill and Philiphaugh —what memories of love and death, of faith and wrong, of blood and of tears they carry ! Always by Yarrow the comely youth goes forth, only to fall by the sword, fighting against odds in the ' Dowie Dens,' or to be caught and drowned in the treacherous pools of this fateful river ; always the woman is left to weep over her lost and ' lealfu' lord.' In the Dow Glen it is the ' Border Widow,' upon whose bower the ' Red Tod of Falkland ' has broken and slain her knight, whose grave she must dig with her own hands :

> ' I took his body on my back,
> And whiles I gaed and whiles I sat ;

I digged a grave and laid him in,
And happed him wi' the sod sae green.

But think nae ye my heart was sair
When I laid the moul's on his yellow hair;
O think nae ye my heart was wae
When I turned about awa' to gae.

Nae living man I 'll love again,
Since that my lovely knight is slain;
Wi' ae lock o' his yellow hair
I 'll chain my heart for evermair.'

An echo of this, but blending with poignant grief a masculine note of rage and vengeance, is the lament of Adam Fleming for Burd Helen, who dropped dead in his arms at their trysting-place in 'fair Kirkconnell Lea,' from the shot fired across the Kirtle by the hand of his jealous rival:

'O thinkna ye my heart was sair,
When my love drapt doun and spak nae mair!
There did she swoon wi' meikle care
　　　On fair Kirkconnell Lea.

O Helen fair, beyond compare!
I 'll make a garland o' thy hair
Shall bind my heart for evermair
　　　Until the day I dee.'

Still older, and not less sad and sweet, is the lilt of *Willie Drowned in Yarrow*, the theme amplified, but not improved, in Logan's lyric:

'O Willie 's fair and Willie 's rare,
And Willie wondrous bonnie;
And Willie hecht to marry me
If e'er he married ony.'

Gamrie, in Buchan, contends with the 'Dowie Howms'
as the scene of this fragment; but surely its sentiment
is pure Yarrow:

> 'She sought him east, she sought him west,
>   She sought him braid and narrow;
> Syne in the cleaving o' a craig
>   She found him drowned in Yarrow.'

But best-remembered of the Yarrow Cycle is *The
Dowie Dens.* One cannot analyse the subtle aroma
of this flower of Yarrow ballads. In it the song of
the river has been wedded to its story 'like perfect
music unto noble words.' It is indeed the voice of
Yarrow, chiding, imploring, lamenting; a voice 'most
musical, most melancholy.' A ballad minstrel with a
master-touch upon the chords of passion and pathos,
with a feeling for dramatic intensity of effect that Nature
herself must have taught him, must have left us these
wondrous pictures of the quarrel, hot and sudden; of
the challenge, fiercely given and accepted; of the
appeal, so charged with wild forebodings of evil:

> ' "O stay at hame, my noble lord,
>   O stay at hame, my marrow!
> My cruel kin will you betray
>   On the dowie howms o' Yarrow " ';

of the treacherous ambuscade under Tinnis bank; of
the stubborn fight, in which a single 'noble brand'
holds its own against nine, until the cruel brother
comes behind that comeliest knight and 'runs his body

thorough'; of the yearning and waiting of the 'winsome marrow,' while fear clutches at her heart :

> ' " Yestreen I dreamed a doleful dream,
>   . I fear there will be sorrow,
> I dreamed I pu'ed the birk sae green
>   For my true love on Yarrow.
>
> O gentle wind that blaweth south
>   Frae where my love repaireth,
> Blaw me a kiss frae his dear mouth
>   And tell me how he fareth " ' ;

lastly, of the quest 'the bonnie forest thorough,' until on the trampled den by Deucharswire, near Whitehope farmhouse, she finds the 'ten slain men,' and among them 'the fairest rose was ever cropped on Yarrow' :

> ' She kissed his cheek, she kaimed his hair,
>   She searched his wounds a' thorough,
> She kissed them till her lips grew red
>   On the dowie howms o' Yarrow.'

The story is said to be founded on the slaughter of Walter Scott of Oakwood, of the house of Thirlstane, by John Scott of Tushielaw, with whose sister Grizel the murdered man had, in 1616, contracted an irregular marriage, to the offence of her kin. On this showing, it is of the later crop of the ballads. But it is well-nigh impossible to think of rueful Yarrow flowing through her dens to any other measure than that which keeps repeating

> ' By strength of sorrow
> The unconquerable strength of love.'

But, as Wordsworth reminds us, these ever-youthful waters have their gladsome notes. On the not unchallengeable ground that it makes mention, in one version, of 'St. Mary's' as the fourth Scots Kirk at which halt was made after leaving the English Border, *The Gay Goshawk* has been set down among the Yarrow ballads; and Hogg has confirmed the claim by using the tale as the foundation of his *Flower of Yarrow*. Even here such happiness as the lovers find comes by a perilous way past the very gates of the grave. The feigning of death, as the one means of escape from kinsfolk's ban to the arms of love, was a device known to Juliet and to other heroines of old plays and romances. But few could have abode the test suggested by the 'witch woman' or cruel stepmother, whose experience had taught her that 'much a lady young will do, her ain true love to win':

> ' "Tak' ye the burning lead,
>   And drap a drap on her white bosom
>   To try if she be dead." '

And Lord William, at St. Mary's Kirk, was more fortunate than Romeo in the vault of the Capulets; for when he rent the shroud from the face the blood rushed back to the cheeks and lips, 'like blood-draps in the snaw,' and the 'leeming e'en' laughed back into his own :

> ' "Gie me a chive o' your bread, my love,
>   And ae glass o' your wine,
> For I hae fasted for your love
>   These weary lang days nine." '

The Nut-brown Bride and *Fair Janet* might also be identified as among the Yarrow lays, if only it were granted that there is but one 'St. Mary's Kirk.' In the former, the balladist treats, with dramatic fire and fine insight into the springs of action, the theme that

> 'To be wroth with those we love
> Doth work like madness in the brain.'

As in Barbara Allan, a word spoken amiss sets division between two hearts that had beat as one :

> 'Lord Thomas spoke a word in jest,
> Fair Annet took it ill.'

In haste he consults mother and brother whether he should marry the 'Nut-brown Maid, and let Fair Annet be,' and so long as they praise the tochered lass he scorns their counsel; he will not have 'a fat fadge by the fire.' But when his sister puts in a word for Annet his resentment blazes up anew ; he will marry her dusky rival in despite. With a heart not less hot, we may be sure, his forsaken love dons her gayest robes, and at St. Mary's Kirk she casts the poor brown bride into the shade in dress as well as in looks. Small wonder if the bride speaks out with spite when her bridegroom reaches across her to lay a red rose on Annet's knee. The words between the two angry women are like rapier-thrusts, keen and aimed at the heart. 'Where did ye get the rose-water that maks your skin so white?' asks the bride ; and when Annet's swift retort goes home, she can only respond with the long bodkin drawn from her hair. The word in jest costs the lives of three.

Fair Janet's is another tragic wedding; love, and jealousy, and guilt again hold tryst in the little kirk whose grey walls are scarce to be traced on the green platform above the loch. 'I've seen other days,' says the pale bride to her lost lover as he dances with her bridesmaiden :

> ' " I 've seen other days wi' you, Willie,
>   And so hae mony mae ;
> Ye would hae danced wi' me yoursel'
>   And let a' ithers gae " ' ;

and, dancing, she drops dead.

Fasting, and fire, and sickness unto death were, however, tame ordeals compared with those which 'Burd Helen' came through, as they are described in the ballad Professor Child holds, not without reason, to have 'perhaps no superior' in our own or any other tongue. Patient Grizel, herself the incarnation in literary form of a type of woman's faithfulness and meek endurance of wrong that had floated long in mediæval tradition, might have shrunk from some of the cruel tasks which Lord Thomas—the 'Child Waters' of the favourite English variant—lays upon the mother of his unborn child—the woman whose self-surrender had been so complete that she has not the blessing of Holy Church and the support of wifely vows to comfort her in her hour of trial. All the summer day she runs by his bridle-rein until they come to the Water of Clyde, which 'Sweet Willie and May Margaret' also sought to ford on a similar errand :

> ' And he was never so courteous a knight,
>   As stand and bid her ride ;
>   And she was never so poor a may,
>   As ask him for to bide.'

She stables his steed ; she waits humbly at table as the little page-boy ; she listens, her colour coming and going, to the mother's scorns and the young sister's naïve questions. But never, until the supreme moment of her distress, does she draw one sign of pity or relenting from her harsh lord. Then, indeed, love and, remorse, as if they had been dammed back, break forth like a flood, that bursts the very door, and makes it 'in flinders flee.' And because

> ' The marriage and the kirkin'
>   Were baith held on ae day,'

our simple balladist bids us believe that the twain lived happily ever after.

The variations of this ancient tale, localised in nearly every European country, are innumerable ; and Professor Veitch was disposed to trace them to the thirteenth century *Tale of the Ash*, by Marie of France. The 'Fair Annie' of another ballad on the theme seems to have borrowed both name and history directly from the 'Skiæn Annie' of Danish folk-poetry. Here the old love suffers the like indignity that was thrown upon the too-too submissive Griselda ; she has to make ready the bridal bed for her supplanter and do other menial offices, until a happy chance reveals the fact that the newcomer is her sister. Yet

neither from Fair Annie nor from Burd Helen comes
word of reproach or complaint. The exceeding bitter
thought is whispered only to the heart:

> ' " Lie still, my babe, lie still, my babe,
>   Lie still as lang 's ye may ;
> For your father rides on high horseback,
>   And cares na for us twae." '

And again,

> ' " Gin my seven sons were seven young rats,
>   Runnin' upon the castle wa' ;
> And I were a grey cat mysel',
>   Soon should I worry ane and a'." '

Wide, surely, is the gulf between the Original Woman
of old romance and the New Woman of recent fiction.
The change, no doubt, is for the better ; and yet is it
altogether for the better ?

According to all modern canons, the conduct of
these too-tardy bridegrooms was brutal beyond words ;
and as for the heroines of the Romantic Ballad,
Mother Grundy, had she the handling of them, would
use them worse than ever did moody brother or crafty
stepmother. But the balladists and ballad characters
had their own gauges of conduct. Their morals were
not other or better than the morals of their age. They
strained out the gnats and swallowed the camels of the
law as given to Moses ; perhaps if they could look into
modern society and the modern novel they would
charge the same against our own times and literature.
If they broke, as they were too ready to do, the Sixth
Commandment, or the Seventh, they made no attempt

G

to glose the sin; they dealt not in innuendo or *double entendre*. Beside the page of modern realism, the ballad page is clean and wholesome. Human passion unrestrained there may be; but no sickly or vicious sentiment. There is a punctilious sense of honour; and if it is sometimes the letter rather than the spirit of vow or promise that is kept, the knights and ladies in the ballads are no worse than are the Pharisees of our day; and they are always ready to pay, and generally do pay, the utmost penalty.

Thus, in that most powerful and tragic ballad, *Clerk Saunders*, May Margaret ties a napkin about her eyes that she 'may swear, and keep her aith,' to her 'seven bauld brothers,' that she had not seen her lover 'since late yestreen'; she carries him across the threshold of her bower, that she may be able to say that his foot had never been there. The story of the sleeping twain— the excuses for their sin; the reason why ruth should turn aside vengeance—is told, in staccato sentences, by the brothers as they stand by the bedside of their 'ae sister,' with 'torches burning bright':

> 'Out and spake the first o' them,
>   "I wot that they are lovers dear";
> And out and spake the second o' them,
>   "They've been in love this mony a year";
>
> And out and spake the third o' them,
>   "His father had nae mair than he."'

And so until the seventh—the Rashleigh of the band— who spake no word, but let his 'bright brown brand' speak for him. What follows rises to the extreme height of the balladist's art; literature might be challenged for anything surpassing it in simplicity and power, in the mingling of horror and pathos:

> 'Clerk Saunders he started and Margaret she turned,
>   Into his arms as asleep she lay;
> And sad and silent was the night
>   That was atween the twae.
>
> And they lay still and sleepéd sound,
>   Until the day began to daw,
> And softly unto him she said,
>   "It's time, true love, you were awa'."
>
> But he lay still and sleepéd sound,
>   Albeit the sun began to sheen;
> She looked atween her and the wa',
>   And dull and drumlie were his een.'

In the majority of ballads of the *Clerk Saunders* class there is some base agent who betrays trust and brings death upon the lovers. 'Fause Foodrage' takes many forms in these ancient tales without changing type. He is the slayer of 'Lily Flower' in *Jellon Graeme*; and the boy whom he has preserved and brought up sends the arrow singing to his guilty heart. Lammiken, the 'bloodthirsty mason,' who must have a life for his wage, is another enemy within the house who finds his way through 'steekit yetts'; and he is assisted by the 'fause nourice.' In other ballads it is the 'kitchen-boy,' the 'little foot-page,' the 'churlish carle,' or the bower-woman who plays the spy and tale-bearer. In *Glen-kindie*, 'Gib, his man,' is the vile betrayer of the noble harper and his lady. Sometimes, as in *Gude Wallace*, *Earl Richard*, and *Sir James the Rose*, it is the 'light

leman' who plays traitor.   But she quickly repents, and
meets her fate in the fire or at the sword's point, in
'Clyde Water' or in 'the dowie den in the Lawlands o'
Balleichan.'   In *Gil Morice*, that ballad which Gray
thought 'divine,' it is 'Willie, the bonnie boy,' whom
the hero trusted with his message, that in malice and
wilfulness brings about the tremendous catastrophe of
the tale.   He calls aloud in hall the words he was bid
whisper in the ear of Lord Barnard's lady—to meet Gil
Morice in the forest, and 'speir nae bauld baron's leave.'

> 'The lady stampéd wi' her foot
>   And winkéd wi' her e'e ;
> But for a' that she could say or do
>   Forbidden he wadna be.'

It is the angry and jealous baron who, in woman guise,
meets and slays the youth who is waiting in gude greenwood, and brings back the bloody head to the mother.

Other fine ballads in which mother and son carry on
tragic colloquy are *Lord Randal* and *Edward*.   These
versions of a story of treachery and blood, conveyed in
the dark hints of a strange dialogue, have received many
touches from later hands; but the germ comes down
from the age of tradition.   It has even been noted that,
with the curious tenacity with which the ballad memory
often clings to a detail while forgetting or mislaying
essential fact, the food with which, in the version
Burns recovered for Johnson's *Museum*, Lord Randal
is poisoned—'eels boiled in broo'—is identical with
that given to his prototype in the folk-ballads of Italy

and other countries. The structure of this ballad, like
the beautiful old air to which it is sung, bears marks of
antiquity, and its wide diffusion militates against Scott's
not very convincing suggestion that it refers to the
alleged poisoning of the Regent Randolph. But it
lacks the terrible and dramatic intensity of *Son Davie*,
better known in the version transmitted, under the
name of *Edward*, by Lord Hailes to Bishop Percy's
Reliques. Here it is the murderer, and not the victim,
who answers; and it is the questioning mother, and not
the absent false love, with whom the curse is left as a
legacy. Despair had never a more piercing utterance
than this:

> ' " And what will ye leave to your bairns and your wife ?
> Edward, Edward !
> And what will ye leave to your bairns and your wife
> When ye gang over the sea, O ? "
>
> " The warld 's room, let them beg through life,
> Mither, Mither !
> The warld 's room, let them beg through life,
> For them never mair will I see, O ! "
>
> " And what will ye leave to your ain mither dear ?
> Edward, Edward !
> And what will ye leave to your ain mother dear,
> My dear son, now tell me, O ? "
>
> " The curse o' hell from me shall ye bear,
> Mither, Mither !
> The curse o' hell from me shall ye bear,
> Sic counsels ye gae me, O ! " '

Although Yarrow be the favoured haunt on Scottish
soil—may we not also say on the whole round of earth?
—of the Romantic Ballad, and has coloured them, and

taken colour from them, for all time, yet there are other streams and vales that only come short of being its rivals. 'Leader Haughs,' for instance, which the harp of Nicol Burne, the 'Last Minstrel' who wandered and sang in the Borderland, has linked indissolubly with Yarrow braes, know of ballad strains well-nigh as sweet as those of the neighbour water. But cheerfulness rather than sadness is their prevailing note. *Auld Maitland*, the lay which James Hogg's mother repeated to Scott, has its scene on Leader side, and at the 'darksome town'—a misnomer in these days—of Lauder. Long before the time of that tough champion, St. Cuthbert and True Thomas had wandered and dreamed and sang by Leader. It was a Lord Lauderdale who rode to Traquair to court, after the older fashion, Katherine Janferie :

> ' He toldna her father, he toldna her mither,
>   He toldna ane o' her kin ;
>   But he whispered the bonnie may hersel',
>   And has her favour won.'

He it was, according to the old ballad, who rode to the bridal at the eleventh hour, with four and twenty Leader lads behind him :

> ' " I comena here to fight," he said,
>   " I comena here to play ;
>   But to lead a dance wi' the bonnie bride,
>   And mount and go my way " ' ;

and it was Lord Lochinvar (although 'he who told the story later' has taught us so differently) who played the inglorious part of the deserted bridegroom. Scott himself drank in the passion for Border romance and chivalry on the braes of Sandyknowe, between Leader and Eden waters, not far from Smailholm and Dryburgh, and Huntly Bank and Mellerstain, and Rhymer's Tower and the Broom o' the Cowdenknowes. According to Mr. Ford, the ballad which takes its name from this last-mentioned spot is traditionally assigned to a Mellerstain maid named Crosbie, whose words were set to music by no less famous a hand than that of David Rizzio. So that here at least we have a vague echo of the name of a balladist and of a ballad-air composer. Between them, the maid of Mellerstain and 'Davy' have harmonised most musically, albeit with some touch of moral laxity, the spirit of pastoral and of ballad romance :

> 'The hills were high on ilka side,
>   And the bucht i' the lirk o' the hill,
> And aye as she sang her voice it rang
>   Out ower the head o' yon hill.
>
> There cam' a troop o' gentlemen,
>   Merrily riding by,
> And ane o' them rade out o' the way
>   To the bucht to the bonnie may.'

Nowhere has the ballad inspiration and the ballad touch lingered longer than by Eden and Leader and Whitadder. Lady Grizel Baillie (who also wonned in Mellerstain) had them—

> 'There once was a may and she lo'ed nae men,
>   And she biggit her bonnie bower doun in yon glen '—

and it still lives in Lady John Scott, who has sung of

The Bonnie Bounds of Cheviot as if the mantle of the Border minstrels had fallen upon her.

After all, the ballads of Yarrow and Ettrick, of the Merse and Teviotdale, owe their superior fame as much as anything to the happy chance that the Wizard of Abbotsford dwelt in the midst of them, and seizing upon them before they were forgotten, made them and the localities classical. Other districts have in this way been despoiled to some extent of their proper meed of honour. Fortune as well as merit has favoured the Border Minstrelsy in the race for survival and for precedence in the popular memory. But Galloway, a land pervaded with romance, claims at least one ballad that can rank with the best. *Lord Gregory* has aliases and duplicates without number. But the scene is always Loch Ryan and some castled island within sight of that arm of the sea, whither the love-lorn Annie fares in her boat 'wi' sails o' the light green silk and tows o' taffetie,' in quest of her missing lord:

> '" O row the boat, my mariners,
> And bring me to the land !
> For yonder I see my love's castle
> Close by the salt sea strand." '

Alas ! cold is her welcome as she stands with her young son in her arms, and knocks and calls on her love, while 'the wind blaws through her yellow hair, and the rain draps o'er her chin.' A voice, that seems that of Lord Gregory, bids her go hence as 'a witch or a wil' warlock, or a mermaid o' the flood '; and with a woful heart she turns back to the sea and the storm.

And when he wakes up from boding dreams to find his true love and his child have been turned from his door, it is too late. His cry to the waves is as vain as Annie's cry to that 'ill woman,' his mother, who has betrayed them:

> ' "And hey, Annie, and how, Annie !
> O Annie, winna ye bide ?"
> But aye the mair that he cried Annie,
> The braider grew the tide.
>
> "And hey, Annie, and how, Annie !
> Dear Annie, speak to me !"
> But aye the louder he cried Annie,
> The louder roared the sea.'

The shores and basin of the Forth have also their rowth of ballads; and some of them have, like *The Lass of Lochryan*, the sound of the waves and the salt smell of the sea mingled with their plaintive music. *Gil Morice* has been 'placed' by Carronside—Ossian's 'roaring Carra'—a meet setting for the story. *Sir Patrick Spens* cleaves to the shores of Fife; though some, eager for the honour of the North, have claimed that it is Aberdour in Buchan that is spoken of in the ballad. By the powerful spell of this old rhyme, the king still sits and drinks the blood-red wine in roofless Dunfermline tower; the ladies still haunt the windy headland—Kinghorn or Elie Ness—with 'their kaims intil their hands' waiting in vain the return of their 'good Scots lords'; the wraith of Sir Patrick himself in misty days strides the silver strand under the Hawes Wood, reading the braid letter. Near by is Donibristle; and it keeps the memory of the 'Bonnie Earl of Moray,' slain here, hints the balladist—though history is silent on the point—for pleasing too well the Queen's eye at Holyrood.

Edinburgh, too, draws a good part of its romance from the ballad bard.   Mary Hamilton, of the Queen's Maries, rode through the Netherbow Port to the gallows-foot:

> ' " Yestreen the Queen had four Maries,
> The night she'll hae but three ;
> There was Marie Seton, and Marie Beaton,
> And Marie Carmichael, and me." '

The Marchioness of Douglas wandered disconsolate on Arthur's Seat and drank of St. Anton's well:

> ' " 'O waly, waly, love be bonnie
> A little time while it is new,
> But when it's auld it waxes cauld
> And fades awa' like morning dew.
>
> But had I wist before I kissed
> That love had been so ill to win,
> I'd locked my heart within a kist
> And fastened it wi' a siller pin " ';

and across the hill lies the 'Wells o' Wearie.'   Nowhere else has the wail of forsaken love found such wistful expression—except in *The Fause Lover*:

> ' " But again, dear love, and again, dear love,
> Will you never love me again?
> Alas ! for loving you so well,
> And you not me again." '

From Edinburgh wandered Leezie Lindsay, kilting her coats of green satin to follow her Lord Ronald Macdonald the weary way to the Highland Border ; and to its plainstanes came the faithful Lady of Gicht to ransom her Geordie :

'My Geordie, O my Geordie,
  The love I bear my Geordie !
  For the very ground I walk upon
  Bears witness I lo'e Geordie.'

And these regions of the North have as much of the
'blood-red wine' of ballad romance coursing through
them as Tweedside or Lothian, although it may be of
harsher and coarser flavour.   Space does not allow of
doing justice to the Northern Ballads, some of them
simple strains, made familiar by sweet airs, like *Hunting Tower*, or *Bessie Bell and Mary Gray*, or the *Banks
of the Lomond*; others, and these chiefly from the
wintry side of Cairn o' Mount, 'bleak and bare' as that
wilderness of heather ; still others, and from the same
quarter, gallant, warm-hearted, light-stepping tunes as
ever were sung—*Glenlogie*, for instance :

'There were four-and-twenty nobles
  Rode through Banchory fair ;
  And bonnie Glenlogie
  Was flower o' them there.'

For the most part they are variants, many of them
badly mutilated in the rhymes, that are familiar, under
other names, farther south.   They gather about the
family history and the family trees of the great houses
—the Gordons for choice—planted by Dee and Don
and Ythan, where Gadie runs at the 'back o' Ben-
achie,' and in the Bog o' Gicht ; and they tell of love
adventures and mischances that have befallen the Lords
of Huntly or Aboyne, the Lairds of Drum or Meldrum,
and even the humble Trumpeter of Fyvie.

CHAPTER VI

THE HISTORICAL BALLAD

' It fell about the Lammas tide,
  When the muirmen win their hay,
The doughty Douglas bound him to ride
  Into England, to drive a prey.'
                    The Battle of Otterburn.

THE kindly Scot will not quarrel with the comparative
mythologist who tells him that the superstitions em-
balmed in his ballad minstrelsy are wanderers out of
misty times and far countries—primitive ideas and
beliefs that may have started with his remote ancestors
from the heart of the East, to find harbour in the valleys
of the Cheviots and the islands of the West, or that
have drifted thither with the tide of later inroads. Nor
will he greatly protest when the literary historian
assures him that the plots and incidents in the popular
old rhymes of the frenzies and parlous adventures of
love have been borrowed or adapted from the metrical
and prose romances of the Middle Ages. He can
appreciate in his poetry, as in his pedigree, high and
long descent ; all the more since, as he flatters himself,
whencesoever the seed may have come, it has found
kindly soil, and drawn from thence a strength and

colour such as few other lands and ballad literatures can match.

But to suggest that not even our Historical Songs of fight and of foray against our 'auld enemies' of England are genuine, unalloyed products of the national spirit; to hint that *Kinmont Willie*, *The Outlaw Murray*, or *The Battle of Otterburn* itself is an exotic—that were a somewhat dangerous exercise of the art of analytic criticism, in the presence of a Scottish audience. In truth, no poetry of any tongue or land is more powerfully dominated by the sense of locality—is more expressive of the manners of the time and mood of the race—than those rough Border lays of moonlight rides, on reiving or on rescue bound, and of death fronted boldly in the press of spears or 'behind the bracken bush.' These are not tales of the infancy of a people. Scotland had already attained to something of national unity of blood and of sentiment before they came to birth. For generations and centuries she had to keep her head and her bounds against an enemy as watchful and warlike as herself, and many times as strong. Blows were struck and returned, keen and sudden as lightning. The 'hammer of the Scots,' wielded by the English kings, had smitten, and under its blows the race had been welded together and wrought to a temper like steel, supple upon occasion to bend, but elastic and unbreakable, and with a sharp cutting edge.

Heroes conquered or fell; and sometimes a minstrel

was by to sing the exploit. Patriotism and the joy of combat are leading notes in these Historic Ballads. The annals of Scotland are full of family and clan feuds —the quarrels of kites and crows. But, with a fine and true instinct, the best of these ballads avoid taking account of the bickerings in the household. It is when they sing of 'patriot battles won of old,' where Scot and Southron met, 'red-wat shod,' that the strain rises to its clearest, and 'stirs the heart like the sound of a trumpet.' Nor is it always the events that are most noised in the history-book that are best remembered in the ballads. The old singers and their audiences delighted more in personal episode than in filling a big canvas; their genius was dramatic rather than epic. *Hardyknut*, with its commemoration of the battle of Largs and the Northmen, although accepted by the *literati* of the early Georgian era as a genuine 'antique,' has long been proved to be an imitative production of Lady Wardlaw's. The rhyme which the Scottish maidens sang about Bannockburn is lost. The Wallace group of ballads bears plain marks of spurious intermixture, or later composition. There are no traditional verses preserved in popular memory regarding the disasters of Neville's Cross or of Homildon Hill, where so much good Scots blood soaked an alien sod; or of that shameful day of Solway Moss, about which James the Fifth muttered strange words on his dying-bed. Even the pathetic strain, more lyrical, however, than narrative, in which lament is made for

The Flowers o' the Forest, that were 'wede awa'' at
Flodden, came two centuries later than the woful
battle.

Perhaps it is natural that a warlike people should
sing of their triumphs rather than of their defeats and
humiliations.   But if the old ballads have lost sight
of some great landmarks in the country's chronicle, they
have preserved names and incidents which the duller
pen of history has forgotten or overlooked.   The
breath of poetry passes over the Valley of Bones of the
national annals, and each knight stands up in his place,
a breathing man and a living soul.   They are none the
less real and living for us because Dry-as-dust has mis-
laid the vouchers for their birth and their deeds, and
cannot fit them into their place in his family trees and
chronological tables.

It follows, from the strongly patriotic cast of the
ballads of war and fray, that they should have sprung
up most rankly on the battle-fields and around the peel-
towers of the Borderland.   It was on the line of the
Tweed and of the Cheviots that the long quarrel was
fought out; and thus the Merse, Ettrick Forest, and
Teviotdale; the Debateable Land, Liddesdale, and
Annan Water became the native countries of the songs
of raid and battle.   The 'Red Harlaw'—which has
had its own homespun bard, although of a different
note and fibre from the minstrels of the Border—may
be said to have ended the struggle for the mastery
between Highlands and Lowlands.   From thence on-

ward through the age of ballad-making, there were *spreaghs* and feuds enow upon and within the Highland Line. But, until the time when Jacobitism came to give change of theme and bent, along with change of scene, to the spirit of Scottish romance, none of these local bloodlettings sufficed to inspire a ballad of more than local fame; unless indeed the story drew part of its power to live and to please from other sources besides the mere zest for fighting. In distinction, as we shall see from the typical Border War Lay, in which woman, if her presence is felt at all, is kept in the background, as looker-on or rewarder of the fight, in such Northern tales of raid and spulzie as *The Baron of Bracklay, Edom o' Gordon, The Bonnie House o' Airlie*, or even *The Burning o' Frendraught*, she is brought into the heart of the scene and forms an abiding and controlling influence.

In a word, these are at least as much Romantic as Historical Ballads. We suspect that woman's guile and treachery are at work, as soon as we hear the taunting words of Bracklay's lady:

> ' O rise, my bauld Baron,
>   And turn back your kye,
> For the lads o' Drumwharron
>   Are driving them bye.'

We are made sure of it, when the minstrel tells us :

> ' There was grief in the kitchen
>   But mirth in the ha' ;
> But the Baron o' Bracklay
>   Is dead and awa'.'

And in the assault on the 'House o' the Rhodes,' it is not the wild work of the Gordons on which our thoughts are fixed; it is not even on the Forbeses, riding hard and fast to be in time for rescue:

> 'Put on, put on, my michty men,
> As fast as ye can drie;
> For he that's hindmost o' my men
> Will ne'er get good o' me.'

It is 'the bonnie face that lies on the grass,' and Lady Ogilvie, and not her lord or the 'gleyed Argyll,' is central figure of the tale of the raid of the Campbells against their hereditary foes in Angus.

As a rule, in those ballads of the Borders whose business is with foray and reprisal, we have none of this disturbing element. The sheer love of adventure, the chance of exchanging 'hard dunts' with the Englishmen, is inducement enough for us to follow the lead of the Douglas or Buccleuch across the Waste of Bewcastle or through the wilds of Kidland. The women folks are safe and well defended in the peel-towers, from whence, when the word has gone out to 'warn the water speedilie,' the bale-fires flash up the dales from water-foot to well-e'e, and set the hill-crests aflame with the news of the enemy's coming. They may have given the hint of a toom larder by serving a dish of spurs on the board. They will be the first to welcome home the warden's men or the moss-troopers if they return with full hands, or to rally them if they have brought nothing back but broken heads. But keeping or breaking the peace on the Borders is a man's part; and only men mingle in it. Both sides are too accustomed to surprises, and have too many strong fortalices and friends at hand, to give the foe the chance of 'lifting' whole families as well as their gear and cattle. The last thing one looks for, then, in the moss-trooping ballads is a strain of tender and pathetic sentiment. The tone is hearty and virile even to boisterousness. The minstrel, like the fighters, revels in hard knocks and rough jests. He has ridden with them probably, and has had the piper's share of the plunder and whatever else was going. He has heard 'the bows that bauldly ring and the arrows whiddering near him by,' as he passes through the 'derke Foreste.' He took the fell with the other folk in the following of the Scottish warden, and looking down the slope towards Reed Water, witnessed the beginning and end of the skirmish known as *The Raid of the Reidswire.*

> 'Be this our folk had taen the fell
>   And planted pallions there to bide;
> We looked down the other side,
>   And saw them breasting ower the brae
> Wi' Sir John Forster as their guide,
>   Full fifteen hundred men and mae.'

With strokes, graphic and humorous, he describes how the meeting of the two wardens, 'begun with merriment and mowes,' turned to the exchange of such 'reasons rude' between Tyndale and Jed Forest, as flights of arrows and 'dunts full dour.' Pride was at the bottom of the mischief; pride and the memory of old scores.

> ' To deal with proud men is but pain ;
>   For either must ye fight or flee,
>   Or else no answer make again,
>   But play the beast and let them be.'

And so, when the English raised the question of surrendering a fugitive,

> ' Carmichael bade them speak out plainlie,
>   And cloak no cause for ill or good ;
>   The other answering him as vainly,
>   Began to reckon kin and blood ;
>   He raise, and raxed him where he stood,
>   And bade him match him wi' his marrows ;
>   Then Tyndale heard these reason rude,
>   And they let off a flight of arrows.'

Again, in *Kinmont Willie*, the flower, with one exception to be named, of the ballads that celebrate the exploits of the 'ruggers and rivers,' the singer lets slip, as it were by accident, that he was of the bold and lawless company that broke Carlisle Castell in time of peace. The old lay tingles and glows with the restless untameable courage, the dramatic fire, the grim humour, and the spirit of good fellowship that were characteristic, along with some less admirable qualities, of the old Borderers. The rage, tempered with a dash of Scots caution, of the Bauld Buccleuch when he heard that his unruly countryman had been taken 'against the truce of border tide' by the 'fause Sakelde and the keen Lord Scroope'; his device for a rescue that while it would set the Kinmont free, would 'neither harm English lad nor lass,' or break the peace between the countries; the keen questionings and adroit replies that passed, like thrust and parry, between the divided bands of the warden's men and Sakelde himself, who met them successively as they crossed the Debateable Land, until it came to the turn of tongue-tied Dickie o' Dryhope, who, having never a word ready, 'thrust the lance through his fause bodie,'—all these are told in the most vigorous and graphic style of rough first-hand narrative. And then the story-teller takes up the parable in his own person, and describes how he and his comrades plunged through the flooded Eden, climbed the bank, and through 'wind and weet and fire and sleet' came beneath the castle wall :—

> 'We crept on knees and held our breath,
>   Till we placed the ladders against the wa';
> And sae ready was Buccleuch himsel'
>   To mount the first before us a'.
>
> He's ta'en the watchman by the throat,
>   And flung him down upon the lead—
> "Had there not been peace between our lands,
>   Upon the other side thou 'dst gaed !"'

In the 'inner prison' lay Willie o' Kinmont, like a wolf in a trap, sleeping soft and waking oft, with thoughts of the gallows, on which he was to swing in the morning, and of his wife and bairns and the 'gude fellows' in the Debateable Land he was never to see again. But in an instant, at the hail and sight of his friends, the fearless humour of the Border rider comes back to him; mounted, irons and all, on the shoulders of Red Rowan, 'the starkest man in Teviotdale,' he must first take farewell of his host, Lord Scroope, with a significant promise that he would 'pay him lodging maill when first they met on the border side.'

> 'Then shoulder high, with shout and cry,
>   We bore him down the ladder lang ;
> At every stride Red Rowan made
>   I wot the Kinmont's airns played clang.
>
> "O mony a time," quo' Kinmont Willie,
>   " I 've ridden a horse baith wild and wud ;
> But a rougher beast than Red Rowan
>   I ween my legs have ne'er bestrode." '

Then comes the wild rush for the Eden, where it flowed from bank to brim, with all Carlisle streaming behind in chase, and the bold plunge of the fugitives into the spate, leaving Lord Scroope staring after them, sore astonished, from the water's edge:

> ' " He's either himsel' a devil frae hell,
>   Or else his mither a witch maun be ;
> I wadna' have ridden that wan water
>   For a''the gowd in Christentie." '

History attests the main incidents and characters of *Kinmont Willie* as true to the facts; and tradition has broidered the story with incidents which the ballad itself does not record. The daughter of the smith, on the road between Longtown and Langholm, used to relate, half a century afterwards, how Buccleuch impatiently thrust his spear through the window to arouse her father and rid Armstrong's legs from their 'cumbrous spurs,' and remembered seeing the rough riders grouped in the outer darkness and streaming

with wet.   The rescue was one of the latest of the
episodes of Border warfare before the Union of the
Crowns; and Armstrong of Kinmont himself, besides
being a typical specimen of his clan,

> ' Able men,
> Somewhat unruly, and very ill to tame,'

was one of the last of what we may describe as the
legitimate line of Border freebooters, before the freebooter became merged in the vulgar thief, as explained
quaintly and sympathetically in Scott of Satchells'
rhyme:

> ' It 's most clear a freebooter doth live in hazard's train;
> A freebooter 's a cavalier who ventures life for gain;
> But since King James the Sixth to England went,
> There has been no cause for grief;
> And he that hath transgressed since then,
> Is no cavalier, but a thief.'

No doubt many other like exploits of, capture and
rescue were enacted and recounted on the Borders in
the troublous times. *Jock o' the Side* and *Archie o'
Ca'field* read almost like variants of *Kinmont Willie.*
Their heroes, too, are 'notour lymours and thieves,'
living on or near the margin of the Debateable Land;
and he of the Side, in particular, lives in Sir Richard
Maitland's bede-roll of the Liddesdale thieves, as only
'too well kend' by his peaceable neighbours,

> ' A greater thief did never hyde;
> He never tyris
> For to brek byris,
> Owre muir and myris,
> Owre gude and guide.'

Both are clapped into 'prison strang,' and liberated by a night raid and surprise. But the scene of rescue is shifted from Carlisle to Newcastle in the one case, and to Dumfries Tolbooth in the other. Hobbie Noble, the English outlaw, performs for the redoubtable Jock o' the Side the service rendered by Red Rowan; and 'mettled John Hall o' laigh Teviotdale' clatters down the Tolbooth stairs with Archie Armstrong of the Calfhill on his back, to mount him on his fleet black mare. And from the safe side of Tyne and of Nith, instead of Eden, they send their jeers and challenges back at the discomfited English pursuers. The old balladists may have mixed up places, names, and incidents in their memories, as they were rather wont to do, and laid skaith or credit at the wrong doors. But while their poetic and dramatic merit may vary, the spirit of the very baldest of these ancient songs is irresistible. The Border reiver may play a foul trick in the game; the Armstrongs, for instance, requited scurvily the services of Hobbie Noble, 'the man that lowsed Jock o' the Side;' but the roughest of these tykes, whether they rode behind the Captain of Bewcastle or the Laird of Buccleuch or Ferniehirst, or fought for their own hand, had their own code of honour, and the balladist zealously and jealously measures by it their acts and words. The worst of them had courage; they snap their fingers and laugh in the very teeth of death. Hobbie Noble, with the can of beer at his lips and the rope about his neck, could sing with an approving conscience—

> ' "Now, fare thee well, sweet Mangerton,
>   For ne'er again I will thee see ;
>   I wad hae betrayed nae man alive
>   For a' the gowd in Christentie " '—

a farewell that reminds us of that of the Highland cateran, Macpherson, who 'so rantingly, so dantonly,' played a spring and danced to it beneath the gallows-tree at Banff, crying out the while against 'treacherie,' and broke his fiddle across his knee when none among the crowd would take it from his hand.

Like Sir Lancelot, in the famous eulogy of Sir Ector, these Borderers of old were not only strong men of their hands, but strong also of heart, and 'true friends to their friends,' who, since they held the first line of defence of the Kingdom, might be said to embrace, after their own family and clan, their countrymen at large. They might, on occasion, 'seek their broth in England and in Scotland both.' But they robbed and slew, when it was possible, with patriotic discrimination. In *Johnie Armstrong* and *The Sang o' the Outlaw Murray* the heroes take credit for their 'honesty' and for their services to their country. The former boasts that 'never a Scots wife could have said that e'er I skaithed her ae puir flee'; and the other that he had won Ettrick Forest from the Southron without help from king or noble. Yet the quarrel of both is with the Scottish sovereign, who has come South intent on the exemplary and kingly work of 'making the rash bush keep the cow'; and, stranger still, it is for the bold-

spoken outlaws, and not for the legitimate guardian of
Border peace, that the minstrel engages our sympathies.

If we may credit the surmises of Mr. P. Macgregor
Chalmers, the Outlaw Murray is none other than the
'John Morvo,' the builder who has set an admirable
mark of his own upon Melrose Abbey and other ecclesiastical fanes, and, as Sheriff of the Forest, built Newark
Castle after he had, in jest or earnest, defied the authority of his patron, King James IV.; perhaps he was even
the writer of the ballad. This is a pretty strong order
on our faith; although it must be confessed that there
is a singular mixture, in this fine old lay, of information
on architecture, venerie, and local ownership of land;
and the Outlaw is made to have all the best of the combat of wits and words, and of the bargain with which it
ends. 'Name your lands,' cries the King, 'where'er
they lie, and here I render them to thee'; and the
Outlaw promptly responds:

> ' " Fair Philiphaugh is mine by right,
>   And Lewinshope still mine shall be,
> Newark, Foulshiels, and Tinnis baith,
>   My bow and arrow purchased me.
>
> And I have native steads to me,
>   And some by name I do not knaw;
> The Hangingshaw and Newark Lee,
>   And mony mair in the Forest shaw." '

Very different was the guerdon which Johnie Armstrong of Gilnockie got from King James the Fifth,
when, in an evil hour, he came with a gallant company
from his stronghold in Eskdale to meet that monarch,

who had ridden with a strong force into the heart of
the moss-troopers' country, intent on taming the march-
men.   Well might the ladies 'look from their loft
windows,' and sigh, 'God bring our men weel hame
again!' as Johnie, and the six-and-thirty Armstrongs
and Elliots in his train, ran their horses through Langholm howm in their haste to welcome their 'lawful
king.'   This expedition of 1529 has left its mark on
ballad poetry as well as history; through the hanging
of Cockburn of Henderland it gave occasion for the
Lament of the Border Widow.   But no incident in it
made deeper impression on the popular memory—
none seems to have caused more sorrow and reprobation—than the stringing up of the Laird of Gilnockie
and his followers on the trees at Carlenrig, at the head
of Teviot.   A 'Johnie Armstrong's Dance' was popular
when the *Complaynt of Scotland* was written twenty
years later; and Sir David Lyndsay, in one of his plays,
makes his Pardoner hawk about, among his relics of
saints, the cords of good hemp that hanged the un-
lucky laird of Gilnockie Hall, with the commendation
that

> 'Wha'ever beis hangit in this cord
>   Neidis never to be drowned.'

At the bar of judgment of the balladists, the deed was
counted murder:

> 'Scotland's heart was ne'er sae wae
>   To see sae mony brave men die';

and murder all the less pardonable, since the king who

ordered it was himself an inspirer and, as some say, a writer of ballads. As is pointed out in the *Border Minstrelsy*, the ballad, in its account of the interview between the king and his troublesome subject, follows pretty closely the narrative of Pitscottie. 'What wants that knave that a king should have?' was the offended remark of James, when he saw the band approaching him in the bravery of their war-gear. And Johnie, when all his appeals and bribes proved to be vain, could also speak a frank word:

> '"To seek het water beneath cauld ice,
>   Surely it is a great follie;
> I have asked grace at a graceless face,
>   But there is nane for my men and me."'

Whatever their misdeeds, Gilnockie and his men had certainly hard measure and short shrift. The king's courtiers, it is alleged, incited him to make a summary end of the Armstrongs; and he had not the biting answer ready which his father is said to have given to the 'keen laird of Buccleuch,' when that Border chieftain urged him to 'braid on with fire and sword' against the Outlaw of Ettrick Forest:

> 'Now haud thy tongue, Sir Walter Scott,
>   Nor speak of reif or felonie;
> For had every honest man his coo,
>   A right puir clan thy name would be.'

But when their own clan or dependants made appeal for help or vengeance, none were more prompt with the strong word and deed than the Scotts—witness, *Kinmont Willie*; witness also, *Jamie Telfer o' the Fair*

Dodhead. When Jamie ran hot-foot to Branksome Hall with the news that the Captain of Bewcastle had ramshackled his house and driven his gear and stock, until

> 'There was naught left in the Fair Dodhead
> But a greeting wife and bairnies three,'

did not Buccleuch start up like an old roused lion?

> ' "Gar warn the water, braid and wide,
> Gar warn it soon and hastilie !
> They that winna ride for Telfer's kye,
> Let them never look on the face o' me ! " '

And the chase goes on, from the Dodhead on the Ettrick until, at the fords of the Liddel, the enemy are brought to bay; and we have the fine picture of Auld Wat of Harden, the husband of the 'Flower of Yarrow,' and a forebear of the author of *Waverley*, as he 'grat for very rage' when Willie Scott, the son of his chief, lay slain by an English stroke:

> 'But he 's ta'en aff his good steel cap,
> And thrice he 's waved it in the air.
> The Dinley's snaw was ne'er mair white
> Than the lyart locks of Harden's hair.'

Vain was the offer by the Bewcastle raiders to men in such mood to take back the cattle that had been lifted:

> 'When they cam' to the Fair Dodhead,
> They were a welcome sight to see !
> For instead of his ain ten milk-kye,
> Jamie Telfer has gotten thirty-and-three.'

Auld Maitland treats of an inroad on the opposite side of the country, of more ancient date and more formidable character. Its hero appears to have been a progenitor of that line of Lethington in East Lothian, and of Thirlstane, in Lauderdale, who, planted firmly on both sides of Lammermuir, produced in after-times warriors, statesmen, and even poets of note. Gavin Douglas places Maitland, with the 'auld beird grey,' among the legendary inmates of his 'Palace of Honour'; and Scott identifies him as a Sir Richard de Mautlant who, in the latter half of the thirteenth century, and probably during the Wars of Independence, held the ancestral lands by Leaderside, on the track of invading armies crossing the Tweed between Coldstream and Melrose, and holding in to Lothian by Soultra Hill. Accordingly, the ballad tells us that the English army, under King Edward, assembled on the Tyne:

> 'They lighted on the banks of Tweed,
>   And blew their fires so het,
> And fired the Merse and Teviotdale
>   All in an evening late.
>
> As they flared up o'er Lammermuir
>   They burned baith up and down,
> Until they came to a darksome house,
>   Some call it Lauder town.'

Many a foray from the same direction followed the same gait, their coming heralded by the bale-fires that flashed the signal from Hume Castle to Edgarhope (wrongly identified by Professor Veitch with Edgerston on Jed Water), and from Edgarhope to Soultra Edge. But memorable above all other Border raids recorded

in song or story, is that encounter in which 'the
Douglas and the Percy met,' and which has inspired
perhaps the very finest of the historical ballads of each
country.   Moot points there are of locality, date, and
circumstances; but it is generally accepted that the
rhyme known for many centuries in Scotland as *The
Battle of Otterburn*, and the English *Chevy Chase* are
versions, from opposite sides, of one event—a skirmish
fought in the autumn of 1388 on Rede Water, between
a band of Scots, under James, Earl of Douglas, return-
ing home laden with spoil, and a body of English, led
by Hotspur, the son of the Earl of Northumberland,
in which Douglas was slain and young Harry Percy
taken prisoner.   It were as hard to decide between the
merits of these famous old lays as to award the prize
for prowess between the respective champions.   But
it may be noted, as a fine Borderer's trait, that each
of the two ballads does full justice to the chivalry and
fighting mettle of the enemy.   It is to be observed also
that they are different poems, and not merely versions
of the same; and that *The Battle of Otterburn* and
the other racy and vigorous ballads of its class dealt
with in this chapter, are of themselves sufficient to
refute the arrogant dictum of Mr. Carew Hazlitt, that
Scotland has no original ballad-poetry to speak of,
and that what she calls her own are 'chiefly English
ballads, sprinkled with Northern provincialisms.'

But while they are, as Scott says, different in essen-
tials, the English and Scottish ballads have exchanged

phrases and even verses, as the English and Scottish warriors exchanged strokes, and these of the best :

> ' When Percy wi' the Douglas met,
>   I wat they were full fain ;
> They swakked their swords till sair they swet,
>   And the blood ran doon like rain,'

may lack some of the picturesqueness of the corresponding passage of *Chevy Chase*. But nothing, at least in Scottish eyes, can surpass the simple majesty and pathos of the last words of Douglas—words that sound all the sadder since Walter Scott repeated them, when he also had almost fought his last battle and was wounded unto death :

> ' " My nephew good," the Douglas said,
>   What recks the death o' ane ?
>   Last night I dreamed a dreary dream,
>   And I ken the day's thy ain.
>
> " My wound is deep, I fain would sleep ;
>   Take thou the vanward o' the three,
> And hide mie by the bracken bush
>   That grows upon the lily lee.
>
> " O bury me by the bracken bush,
>   Beneath the blooming brier ;
> Let never living mortal ken
>   A kindly Scot lies here.'

The Historical Ballad of Border chivalry touches its highest and strongest note in these words; they will stand, like Tantallon, proof against the tooth of Time as long as Scotland has a heart to feel and ears to hear.

CHAPTER VII

CONCLUSION

Though long on Time's dark whirlpool tossed,
The song is saved ; the bard is lost.

The Ettrick Shepherd.

BALLAD poetry is a phrase of elastic and variable meaning. In the national repertory there are Ballads Satirical, Polemical, and Political, and even Devotional and Doctrinal, of as early date as many of the songs inspired by the spirit of Love, War, and Romance. Among them they represent the diverse strands that are blended in the Scottish character—the sombre and the bright; the prose and the poetry. The one or the other has predominated in the expression of the genius of the nation in verse, according to the circumstances and mood of the time. But neither has ever been really absent ; they are the opposite sides of the same shield. It is not proposed to enter here into the ballad literature of the didactic type—the ' ballads with a purpose '—either by way of characterisation or example. In further distinction from the authors of the specimens of old popular song, the writers of many or most of them are known to us, at least by name, and are among the most honoured and familiar in our literature.

128

Towards the unlettered bards of the traditional ballads, who 'saved other names, but left their own unsung,' the more serious and self-conscious race of poets who wrote satire and allegory and homily on the same model have generally thought themselves entitled to assume an attitude of superiority and even of disapproval. The verse of those self-taught rhymers was rude and simple, and wanting in those conventional ornaments, borrowed from classic or other sources, which for the time being were the recognised hallmarks of poesy; the moral lessons it taught were not apparent, nor even discoverable. It is curious to note how early this tone of reprobation, of contempt, or at best of kindly condescension on the part of the official priesthood of letters towards the humble tribe of balladists asserts itself, and how long it endures.

Even Edmund Spenser, as quoted by Scott in the *Minstrelsy*, reproves the Irish bards and rhymsters, as he might have done their Scottish brethren, because 'for little reward or the share of a stolen cow' they 'seldom use to choose the doings of good men for the arguments of their poems,' but, on the contrary, those of such men as live 'lawlessly and licentiously upon stealths and spoyles,' whom they praise to the people, and set up as an example to young men. A poetaster of the beginning of the seventeenth century prays his printer that his book 'be not with your Ballads mixt,' and that 'it come not brought on pedlars' backs to common Fairs'—a prayer fulfilled to the letter. And

I

down even to our own century, a host of collectors,
adaptors, and imitators have spoken patronisingly of
the elder ballads, and foisted on them additions and
ornaments that have not always or often been improve-
ments.

The whirligig of time has brought in its revenges;
and the final judgment passed by posterity upon the
respective claims of the formal verse and the 'unpre-
meditated lay' of earlier centuries, has in large measure
reversed that of the age in which they were born. The
former, and particularly where it undertook to scourge
the vices, the heresies, and the follies of the period,
lacks entirely that air of simplicity and spontaneity—
that 'wild-warlock' lilt, that 'wild happiness of thought
and expression'—which, in the phrase of Robert Burns,
marks 'our native manner and language' in ballad
poetry certainly not less than in lyrical song. The
laureated bard, honoured of the Court and blessed by
the Church, is deposed from his pride of place, in the
affections and remembrance of the people at least, while
the chant of the unknown minstrel of 'the hedgerow
and the field' goes sounding on in deeper and widening
volume through the great heart of the race, and is hailed
as the one true ballad voice.

Among the subjects which the Moral and Satirical
Ballad selected for censure were, it will be seen, the
themes and the heroes of the humble broadsheets sung
at the common fairs and carried in the pedlar's pack.
Nor are we to wonder at this. Much of the contents

of that pack is better forgotten.   Much even of what has been preserved might have been allowed to drop into oblivion, without loss to posterity and with gain to the character and reputation of the 'good old times.' The balladists—those of the early broadsheets at least —could be gross on occasion; although, it must be owned, not more gross than the dramatists of Elizabethan and Restoration times, and even the novelists of last century, sometimes deigned to be. In particular, they made the mistake, of venerable date and not quite unknown to this day, of confounding humour with coarseness.   A humorous ballad is usually a thing to be fingered gingerly. Yet, although (partly for the reason hinted at) humour has been said not to be a strongly marked element of the flower of our ballad poetry, there are many of the best of them that have imbedded in them a rich and genuine vein of comic wit or broad fun ; and there are also what may be classed as Humorous Ballads proper (or improper as the case may be), which reflect more plainly and frankly, perhaps, than any other department of our literature, the customs, character, and amusements of the commonalty, and have exercised an important influence on the national poets and poetry of a later day.

Of the blending of the humorous with the romantic, an excellent example is found in the ballad of *Earl Richard and the Carl's Daughter*. The Princess, disguised in beggar's duds, keeps on the hook the deluded and disgusted knight, who has unwillingly taken her up behind him, and with wilful and lively wit draws for him pictures of the squalid home and fare with which she is familiar, until it is her good time and pleasure to undeceive him :

> 'She said, "Good-e'en, ye nettles tall,
>   Where ye grow at the dyke ;
> If the auld carline my mother was here
>   Sae weel 's she wad ye pike.
>
> How she wad stap ye in her poke,
>   I wot she wadna fail ;
> And boil ye in her auld brass pan,
>   And o' ye mak' good kail."
>
> .   .   .   .
>
> " Awa', awa', ye ill woman,
>   Your vile speech grieveth me ;
> When ye hide sae little for yoursel'
>   Ye 'll hide far less for me."
>
> "Gude-e'en, gude-e'en, ye heather berries,
>   As ye grow on yon hill ;
> If the auld carline and her bags were here,
>   I wot she would get her fill.
>
> Late, late at night I knit our pokes,
>   Wi' four-and-twenty knots ;
> And in the morn, at breakfast-time
>   I 'll carry the keys o' your locks."
>
> .   .   .   .
>
> " But if you are a carl's daughter,
>   As I take you to be,
> Where did you get the gay clothing
>   In greenwood was on thee ? "
>
> " My mother she 's a poor woman,
>   But she nursed earl's children three,
> And I got it from a foster-sister,
>   To beguile such sparks as thee."'

Of the ballads descriptive of old country sports and merry-making that have come down to us, the most famous are *Christ's Kirk on the Green* and *Peblis to the Play*. They lead us back to times when life in Scotland was not such a 'serious' thing as it afterwards became —when, under the patronage of the Court or of the Church, Miracle-plays or Moralities were played on the open sward in such places of resort for gentle and simple as Falkland and Stirling and Peebles and Cupar; and the strain of the more solemn mumming was relieved for the benefit of the common folks, by rough jests, horse-play, and dancing, in which their betters freely joined. No doubt it was a piece of sage church and state policy to keep the minds of the people off the dangerous questions that began to be stirring in them, by aid of these scenes of 'dancing and derray,' and of almost Rabelaisian fits of mirth and laughter, the savour of which remained long after they had been placed under the ban of a sterner ecclesiastical rule.

Leslie in Fife and Leslie in Aberdeen are competitors for having given the inspiration to *Christ's Kirk on the Green*, to which Allan Ramsay afterwards added a second part in the same vein. But whether these passages of boisterous merriment, in which 'licht-skirtit lasses and girning gossips' play their part happed under the green Lomond or at Dunideer, there can be no question of the national popularity which the piece long enjoyed. Pope declared that a Scot would fight in his day for its superiority over English ballads; and the

author of *Tullochgorum*, in a letter to Robert Burns,
tells us that at the age of twelve he had it by heart, and
had even tried to turn it into Latin verse.   In *Peblis to
the Play*, the fun is not less nimble although it is a
whit more restrained; there is an infectious spirit of
spring-time and gaiety in the strain that sings of the
festal gathering at Beltane, when burgesses and country
folks fared forth 'be firth and forest,' all 'graithed full
gay' to take part in the sports.   'All the wenches of
the west' were up and stirring by cock-crow, selecting,
rejecting, or comparing their tippets, hoods, and curches.
Not only Peebles, but

> 'Hop-Kailzie, and Cardronow,
>   Gaderit out thick-fald,
> With "Hey and how rohumbelow"
>   The young folk were full bald.
> The bag-pipe blew, and they out-threw
>   Out of the townis untald,
> Lord, what a shout was them amang
>   Quhen thai were ower the wald
>   Their west
> Of Peblis to the play!'

From a phrase used by John Major, it has been suggested that James I. of Scots was the writer of this
poem; and a note on the Bannatyne MS. of *Christ's
Kirk* attributes that companion poem to the same royal
authorship.   In spite of the adverse judgment pro-
nounced by Professors Guest and Skeat, it does not
seem an inconceivable thing that the monarch who
wrote the *King's Quair*, and whose daughter kissed the

lips of Alain Chartier as the reward of France for his sweet singing, should have written these strains descriptive of rural jollity in localities where the court and sovereign are known to have often resorted for hunting and other diversion. The cast and language of the poems appear, however, to belong to a later date; and the quaint stanza, afterwards employed in a modified form with such effect by Fergusson and Burns, is that used by Alexander Scot in *The Justing at the Drum*, and in other burlesque pieces of the early or middle period of the sixteenth century.

A much more taking tradition is that which assigns them to the adventure-loving 'Commons King,' James v. They are thoroughly after the humour'—using the word in the Elizabethan as well as in the ordinary sense—of the wandering 'Red Tod'; who has also been held to be the inspirer, if not the author, of those excellent humorous ballads—among the best of their kind to be found in any language—*The Gaberlunzie Man* and *The Jolly Beggar*.

From the moral point of view, these pieces may, perhaps, come under Spenser's condemnation of the rhymers who sing of amatory adventures in which love is no sooner asked than it is granted. But the balladist carries everything before him by the verve and good humour and pawky wit of his song. There are touches worthy of the comedy spirit of Molière in the description, in *The Gaberlunzie Man*, of the good-wife's alternate blessing and banning as she makes her morning discoveries about the 'silly poor man' whom she has lodged over night :

> 'She gaed to the bed whair the beggar lay ;
> The strae was cauld, he was away ;
> She clapt her hands, cry'd, "Dulefu' day !
>   For some of our gear will be gane."
>
> Some ran to coffer and some to kist,
> But nought was stown that could be mist,
> She danced her lane, cry'd, "Praise be blest,
>   I 've lodg'd a leal poor man.
> Since naething awa, as we can learn,
> The kirn 's to kirn, and milk to yearn,
> Gae but the house, lass, and waken my bairn,
>   And bid her come quickly ben."
>
> The servant gaed where the dochter lay—
> The sheets were cauld, she was away ;
> And fast to the goodwife did say
>   "She 's aff wi' the gaberlunzie man."
> "O fy gar ride, and fy gar rin,
> And haste ye, find these traitors again ;
> For she 's be burnt, and he 's be slain,
>   The wearifu' gaberlunzie man."'

The Jolly Beggar is a variation of the same tale from the book of the moonlight rovings of the 'Guidman o' Ballengeich,' with the same vigour and lively humour, and with the bloom of the old ballad minstrelsy upon it besides :

> 'He took his horn from his side,
>   And blew baith loud and shrill,
> And four-and-twenty belted knights
>   Came skipping o'er the hill.
>
> And he took out his little knife,
>   Loot a' his duddies fa' ;
> And he stood the brawest gentleman
>   That was amang them a'.'

Other excellent specimens of old Scottish humour have come down to us in ballad form, some of them made more familiar to our ears in modernised versions or paraphrases in which, along with the roughnesses, much of the force and quaint drollery of the originals has been smoothed away. Of such is *The Wyf of Auchtermuchty*, a Fife ballad, full of local colour and character, the production of 'Sir John Moffat,' a sixteenth century priest, who loved a merry jest, and of whom we know barely more than the name. With so many other precious fragments of our national poetry, it is preserved in the collection of George Bannatyne, the namefather of the Bannatyne Club, who beguiled the tedium of his retirement in time of plague by copying down the popular verse of his day. It is the progenitor of *John. Grumlie*, and gives us a lively series of pictures of the housewifery and the husbandry, as well as the average human nature of the time, class, and locality to which it belongs. The proverb, 'The more the haste the less the speed,' has never been more humorously illustrated than in the troubles of the lazy guidman who 'weel could tipple oot a can, and neither lovit hunger nor cauld,' and who fancied that he could more easily play the housewife's part:

> 'Then to the kirn that he did stour,
>   And jumbled at it till he swat;
> When he had jumblit ane lang hour,
>   The sorrow crap of butter he gat.
>
> Albeit nae butter he could get,
>   Yet he was cumbered wi' the kirn;
> And syne he het the milk ower het,
>   That sorrow spark o' it wad yearn.'

Of the same racy domestic type are the still popular, *The Barrin' o' the Door, Hame cam' oor Guidman at e'en*, to which, with needless ingenuity, it has been sought to give a Jacobite significance, and *Allan o' Maut*, an allegorical account of the genesis of 'barley bree.' Of this last, also, Bannatyne has noted a version which was probably in vogue in the first half of the sixteenth century. Even the hand of Burns, who has produced, in *John Barleycorn*, the final form of the ballad, could not give us more vigorous and trenchant Scots than is contained in the verses of this venerable rhyme in Jamieson's collection :

> ' He first grew green, syne grew he white,
> Syne a' men thocht that he was ripe ;
> And wi' crookit gullies and hafts o' tree,
> They 've hew'd him down, right dochtilie.
>
> .   .   .   .   .
>
> The hollin souples, that were sae snell,
> His back they loundert, mell for mell,
> Mell for mell, and baff for baff,
> Till his hide flew round his lugs like chaff.'

Three (if not four) generations of the Semples of Beltrees carried the tradition of this homely type of native poetry, with its strong gust and relish of life, and the Dutch-like breadth and fidelity of its pictures of the character and humours of common folk, over the period from the Scottish Reformation to the Revolution ; and are remembered by such pieces as *The Packman's Paternoster, The Piper o' Kilbarchan, The Blithesome Bridal*, and, best and most characteristic of all, *Maggie Lauder*

The 'business of the Reformation of Religion' did not go well with ballad-making or with the roystering fun of the fair and the play. In the stern temper to which the nation was wrought in the struggle to cast out abuses in the faith and practice of the Church and to assert liberty of judgment, the feigned adventures of knights and the sorrows of love-crossed maids seemed to cease for a time to exercise their spell over the fancy of the people. The open-air gatherings and junketings on feast and saints' days, with their attendant mirth and music, were too closely associated with the old ecclesiastical rule, and had too many scandals and excesses connected with them, to escape censure from the new Mentors and conscience-keepers of the nation. When, a little later, the spirit of Puritanism came in, mirth and music, and more particularly the dance, became themselves suspect. They savoured of the follies of this world, and were among the wiles most in use by the Wicked One in snaring souls. The flowers were cut down along with the weeds by those root-and-branch men—only to spring up again, both of them, in due season, more luxuriantly than ever.

There were other and cogent reasons why the exploits of 'Jock o' the Side' and his confreres should be frowned upon and listened to with impatience. The time for Border feud and skirmish was already well-nigh past. Industry and knowledge and the pacific arts of life were making progress. The moss-trooper was already becoming an anachronism and a pestilent nuisance, to be put down by the relentless arm of the law, before the Union of the Crowns. Half a century or more before that event, this opinion had been formed of the reiving clans by their quieter and more thoughtful neighbours, as is manifest from the biting allusions of Sir David Lyndsay and Sir Richard Maitland. But after King James's going to England, even the balladists were chary of lifting up a voice in praise of the freebooters of the former Marches. Men were busy finding and fitting themselves to new ideals of patriotism and duty. The gift and the taste for ballad poetry disappeared, or rather went into retirement for a time, to reappear in other forms at a later call of loyalty and romanticism.

The *Gude and Godlie Ballates* of the Wedderburns had been deliberately produced and circulated by the Reformers, with the avowed intention, as Sheriff Mackay says, of 'driving the old amatory and romantic ballads out of the field, and substituting spiritual songs, set to the same tunes—much as revivalists of the present day have adopted older secular melodies.' But nothing enduring is to be done, in the field of poetry, by mere dint of determination and good intent. If the older songs succumbed for a time to the new spiritual melodies, we may feel sure that it was not without a struggle. On the Borders and in the Highlands, the Original Adam asserted himself, in deed and in song, long after the more sober mind of Fife, Lanark, and the West Country had given itself up to the solution of the new theological and ecclesiastical problems which time and change had brought to the nation. The Reformers complained that the fighting clans of the Western Marches could only with difficulty be induced to turn their thoughts from the hereditary business of the quarrel of the Kingdoms to take up instead the quarrel of the Kirk. Even so late as the Covenanting period, Richard Cameron found it hard work 'to set the fire of hell to the tails' of the Annandale men. They came to the field meetings 'out of mere curiosity, to see a minister preach in a tent, and people sit on the ground' —in a spirit not unlike that in which the people used to gather at *Peblis to the Play* or *Christ's Kirk on the Green,* to mingle a pinch of piety and priestly Moralities with a bellyful of carnal delights. It was not until the preacher had denounced them as 'offspring of thieves and robbers,' that some of them began to 'get a merciful cast.'

This, too, changed in the course of time, and having once caught fire, the religious enthusiasm of the march-men kindled into a brilliant glow, or smouldered with a fervent heat. They flung themselves into the front of Kirk controversy, as they did also into more peaceable pursuits, such as sheep-farming and tweed manufacture, with the same hearty energy which aforetime was expended upon raids into Cumberland and Northumberland.

But through all the changes and distractions of the

three centuries since the Warden's men met with
merriment and parted with blows at the Reidswire, the
old ballad music—the voice of the blood; the very
speech and message of the hills and streams—has
sounded like a softly-played accompaniment to the
strenuous labour of the race with hand and head—a
reminder of the men and the thoughts of 'the days of
other years.' At times, in the strife of Church or State,
or in the chase of gain, the magic notes of this 'Harp
of the North' may have sunk low, may have become
nigh inaudible. But in the pauses when the nation
could listen to the rhythmic beat of its own heart, the
sound has made itself heard and felt like the noise of
many waters or the sough of the wind in the tree-tops;
it is music that can never die out of the land. Its echo
has never been wholly missed by Dee and Earn and
Girvan; certainly never by Yarrow and Teviot and
Tweed. The 'Spiritual Songs'—the 'Gude and Godlie
Ballates'—are lost, or are remembered only by the
antiquary; not indeed because they were spiritual, or
because they were written by worthy men with good
intent—for the Scottish Psalms, sung to their traditional
melodies, touch a still deeper chord in the natural
breast than the ballads—but because they lacked the
sap of life, the beauty and the passion of nature's own
teaching, which only can give immortality to song.
There is a 'Harp of the Covenant, and in it there are
piercing wails wrung from a people almost driven
frantic with suffering and oppression. But the popular

lays of the civil wars and commotions of the seventeenth century are few in number, and singularly wanting in those touches of grace and tenderness and kindly humour that somehow accompany the very roughest and most trenchant of the earlier ballads, like the bloom and fragrance that adorn the bristling thickets of the native whin on the slopes of the Eildons or Arthur Seat. The times were harsh and crabbed, and the song they yielded was like unto themselves. There are ballads of the *Battle of Pentland*, of *Bothwell Brig*, of *Killiecrankie*, and, to make a leap into another century, of *Sheriffmuir*. But they are memorable for the passion of hatred and scorn that is in them, rather than for their merits as poetry—for girdings, from one side or the other, at 'cruel Claver'se' and the red-shanked Highlandmen that slew the hope of the Covenant, or at the

'Riven hose and ragged hools,
Sour milk and girnin' gools,
Psalm beuks and cutty stools'

of Whiggery.

After a time of dearth, however, Scottish poetry began to revive; and one of the earliest signs was the attention that began to be paid to the anonymous ballads of the country. It is curious that the first printed collection of them should have been almost contemporary with that merging of the Parliaments of the two kingdoms, which, according to the fears and beliefs of the time, was to have made an end of the nationality and identity of the smaller and poorer of the countries. It was in 1706—the year before the Union—that James Watson's *Serious and Comic Scots Poems* made their appearance, prompted, conceivably, by the impulse to grasp at what seemed to be in danger of being lost.

Of infinitely greater importance in the history of our ballad literature was the appearance, some eighteen years later, of Allan Ramsay's *Evergreen* and *Tea-Table Miscellany*. It was a fresh dawning of Scottish poetry. Warmth, light, and freedom seemed to come again into the frozen world. The blithe and genial spirit of the black-avised little barber-poet was itself the greatest imaginable contrast to the soured Puritanism and prim formalism that for half a century and more had infested the national letters. But the author of *The Gentle Shepherd* himself—and small blame to him—did not fully comprehend the nature and extent of his mission. He did not wholly rid himself from the prevalent idea that the simple natural turn of the old verse was naked rudeness which it was but decent and charitable to deck with the ornaments of the time before it could be made presentable in polite society; indeed he himself, in later editions especially, tried his hand boldly at emendation, imitation, and continuation.

For a generation or two longer, the ballad suffered from these attentions of the modish muse. Yet the original spark of inspiration was not extinct; in the

Border valleys especially—its native country, as we have called it—there were strains that 'bespoke the harp of ancient days.' Of Lady Grizel Baillie's lilts, composed at 'Polwarth on the Green' or at Mellerstain —classic scenes of song and of legend, both of them— mention has been made; they have on them the very dew of homely shepherd life, closed about by the hills, of 'forest charms decayed and pastoral melancholy.' The Wandering Violer, also, 'Minstrel Burne,' from whom Scott may have taken the hint of the 'last of all the bards who sang of Border chivalry'—caught an echo, in *Leader Haughs*, of the grief and changes 'which fleeting Time procureth.'

> 'For many a place stands in hard case
> Where blyth folks ken'd nae sorrow,
> With Humes that dwelt on Leaderside,
> And Scotts that wonned in Yarrow.'

His song, with its notes of native sweetness and its artificial garnishing of classic allusions, marks the passing of the old ballad style into the new.

Jane Elliot, too, a descendant of that Gibbie Elliot —'the laird of Stobs, I mean the same'—who refused to come to the succour of Telfer's kye, listened to the murmuring of the 'mining Rule' and looked up towards the dark skirt and threatening top of Ruberslaw, as she crooned the old fragment which her fancy shaped into that lilting before daybreak of the lasses at the ewe-milking, turned ere night into wailing for the lost Flowers of the Forest. Her contemporary, Mrs. Cock-

K

burn, who wrote the more hackneyed set of the same Border lament, was of the ancient race of Rutherford of Wauchope in the same romantic Border district,—a district wherein James Thomson, of *The Seasons*, spent his childhood from almost his earliest infancy, and where the prototype of Scott's Dandie Dinmont, James Davidson of 'Note o' the Gate,' sleeps sound under a green heap of turf. To trace the Teviotdale dynasty of song further in the female line, Mrs. Cockburn's niece, Mrs. Scott, was that 'guidwife o' Wauchope-house,' who addressed an ode to her 'canty, witty, rhyming ploughman,' Robert Burns, with an invitation to visit her on the Border—an invitation which the poet accepted, and on the way thither, as he relates, chanced upon 'Esther (Easton), a very remarkable woman for reciting poetry of all kinds, and sometimes making Scots doggerel of her own.'

Meanwhile, in other parts of the country, the search for and the study of the remains of the old and popular poetry was making progress. With this had come a truer appreciation of its beauty and its spirit, and the return of a measure of the earlier gift of spontaneous song. The fancy of Scotland was kindled by the tale of the '45. Her poetic heart beat in sympathy with the 'Lost Cause'—after it was finally lost; even while her reason and judgment remained, on the whole, true to the side and to the principles that were victorious. Men who were almost Jacobin in their opinion—Robert Burns is a prime example—became Jacobite when they donned their singing robes. The faults and misdeeds of the Stewarts were forgotten in their misfortunes. In the gallant but ruinous 'cast for the crown' of the native dynasty, the national lyre found once more a theme for song and ballad. 'Drummossie moor, Drummossie day' drew laments as for another Flodden; and 'Johnnie Cope,' in his flight from the field of Prestonpans, was pursued more relentlessly by mocking rhymes than by Highland claymores.

A rush of Jacobite song, which had the great good fortune to be wedded to music not less witching than itself, followed rather than attended the Rebellion; and has become among the most precious and permanent of the nation's possessions in the sphere of poetry. Whichever side had the better in the sword-play, there can be no doubt which has won the triumph in the piping. Song and music have given the Stewart cause its revenge against fortune; and Prince Charlie, and not Cumberland, will remain for all time the hero of the cycle of song that commemorates the last romantic episode in our domestic annals. Jacobite poetry has been lyrical for the most part. But the ballad— narrative in form and dramatic in spirit—has not been neglected.

In a host of singers, Caroline Oliphant, Baroness Nairne, wears the laurel crown of the Jacobite Muse, and Strathearn is the chief centre of inspiration. But the authoress of *The Auld Hoose*, and *The Land o' the Leal*, also wrote ballads of cheery and pawky, yet

'genty' humour that have caught and held the popular
ear, as witness the immortal *Laird of Cockpen.* Hamilton of Bangour, who was 'out' in the '45, had struck
anew the lyre of Yarrow in *Busk ye, busk ye!* Fife
could already 'cock her crest' over Elizabeth Halkett,
Lady Wardlaw, a balladist whose verse, acknowledged
and unacknowledged, had many genuine touches 'of
the antique manner;' and Lady Anne Barnard, a grand-
daughter of Colin, Earl of Balcarres, whose career was
one of the romances of the '15 and of the House of
Lindsay, was able to tell Sir Walter Scott, so late as
1823, the story of the conception and birth of her *Auld
Robin Gray,* which also, on its first anonymous appearance, was taken by some as 'a very, very ancient
ballad, composed perhaps by David Rizzio.' As with
so many other ballads—perhaps as with most of them
—the inspiration of the words was caught from a
beautiful and still older air—'an ancient Scotch
melody,' says Lady Anne, 'of which I was passionately
fond; Sophy Johnstone used to sing it to us at Balcarres.' The date of this, perhaps the sweetest of our
modern ballads, is fixed approximately by the gifted
writer 'as soon after the close of the year 1771'—
perhaps the first approach that can be made to the
timing a ballad's birth.

Walter Scott, also, was born in the latter half of
1771. Burns was then fifteen years of age, 'beard-
less, young, and blate,' but already, as he wrote to the
'guidwife of Wauchope-house,' with

'The elements o' sang
  In formless jumble right an' wrang
  Wild floating in his brain.'

Already the wish was 'strongly heaving the breast' of
that young Ayrshire ploughman,

'That I, for poor auld Scotland's sake
  Some usefu' plan or beuk could make,
  Or sing a sang at least.'

Galloway had by this time taken up again its rough old
lyre. Away in the North—in the Mearns and in
Buchan, old homes of the ballad—the Reverend John
Skinner had written his genial songs of *Tullochgorum*,
The Ewie wi' the Crookit Horn and the rest, that seem
to thrill with the piercing and stirring notes of fiddle
and pipes, being moved thereto, as he has told us, by
his daughters, 'who, being all good singers, plagued me
for words to their favourite tunes.' Fergusson was
celebrating, in an old stanza, shortly to be made world-
famous, the high jinks on Leith Links. Everywhere,
from the Moray Firth to the Cheviots, and from the
East Neuk of Fife to Maidenkirk, there were preludings
for the new and splendid burst of Scottish song, that
by and by broke from the banks of Ayr and Doon.
The service rendered by the genius of Burns in quick-
ening and purifying Scottish song and ballad poetry has
often been acknowledged. It was, indeed, beyond all
measure and praise. But recognition, has not, perhaps,
been made so fully and frequently of what our 'King

of Song' owed to the popular poetry of country people and elder times—and notably to the ballads—that have been handed down by memory rather than books. His was not an isolated phenomenon, blazing up meteor-like without visible cause or prompting. His poetry is rather the culminating effect of an impulse that had been making itself felt for generations. It was like one of those grand bale-fires of the days of peril and watching, whose sudden gleam made the blood stir in the veins, and turned men's faces skywards, but which caught its message from distant points of light that to us seem almost swallowed in the surrounding darkness.

Burns had an inimitable ear for ballad feeling and for ballad rhythm and music. But, except for some vigorous satiric, political, and bacchanalian chants of his own, and the recasting of a few of the old-fashioned and lively rhymes like *The Carl o' Kellyburn Braes* that were not out of the need of being cleaned and furbished to please a more fastidious age, he could scarcely be called a ballad writer. His special sphere in the restoration and preservation of the old was in lyrical poetry. What Robert Burns achieved for the songs, however, Walter Scott did for the ballads and prose legends of Scotland. The appearance of the *Border Minstrelsy* makes 1802 the red-letter year in the later annals of the Scottish Ballad. More than twenty years before, the little lame boy, with the good blood of two Border clans, the Scotts and the Rutherfords, in his veins, had lain on the braes of Sandyknowe, and had drunk in through all his senses the history and romance of the Borderland. He had heard from the 'aged hind,' or at the 'winter hearth,' the old tales of woe and mirth; wild conjurings of superstition or real events that, although nearer then by a hundred years than they are to-day, had already been magnified, distorted, glorified in passing through the medium of the popular memory. His dreaming fancy did the rest. Looking from his point of vantage across the fair valley of the Tweed to the blue chain of Cheviot, every notch in which was 'a gate and passage of the thief,' every fold below it, the site of some battle or story of old,

> 'Over Tweed's fair flood, and Mertoun's wood,
>   And all down Teviotdale,'

he was able to repeople the scene as it was when ballad romance was not only written but lived:

> 'I marvelled as the aged hind
>   With some strange tale bewitched my mind,
>   Of forayers, who with headlong force
>   Down from that strength had spurred their horse.
>
>   .   .   .   .   .   .
>
>   And ever, by the winter hearth,
>   Old tales I heard of woe or mirth,
>   Of lovers' slights, of ladies charms,
>   Of witches' spells, of warriors' arms;
>   Of patriot battles won of old
>   By Wallace wight and Bruce the bold.'

There could not have been a more 'meet nurse for a poetic child' than the green slopes, the black rocks, and

the grey keep, reflected in its still 'lochan,' of Scott's
ancestral home at Sandyknowe. Dryburgh, Melrose,
Kelso, are hidden in the valley below. The huge
square tower of Hume—'Willie Wastle's' castle—
stands on the same sky-line as Smailholm peel itself,
keeping guard along with it over the passes and
marches of the ancient Scottish Kingdom. Wrang-
holm is near by, where St. Cuthbert dreamed and
played at boyish sports before he set forth on his
mission to christianise Northumbria. Bemerside, the
Broom o' the Cowdenknowes, and the Rhymer's
Tower are not far off; Huntly Bank also, where True
Thomas lay alone listening to the throstle and the jay,
under the Eildon tree, and

> ' Was war of a lady gay
>   Come rydyng ouyr a fair le ' ;

Mellerstain, whence the hero of *James Haitlie* rode to
find favour in the eyes of the king's daughter, and where
Grizel Hume and the Mellerstain Maid afterwards sung
notes as wild and sweet and fresh as ever came from
fairyland; and many a famous spot besides. The
three-headed Eildons are in sight, with Dunion, Ruberslaw, Penielheugh, Minto Crags, Lilliard's Edge,
and all the Border high places. Here Scott's poetic
fancy was born; and he paid it only the tribute that
was its due when he made it the scene of the finest
of the modern ballads of its class, *The Eve of St. John.*
As a shrine of pilgrimage for the lover of ballad lore,
Smailholm and Sandyknowe should rank next after, if

they should not take precedence of the Vale of Yarrow. Six years before Scott's birth, and while Burns was but a toddler, Bishop Percy's *Reliques* had seen the light. The chief gathering-ground of this celebrated collection was on the English side of the Border, and it was not confined to ballad poetry.   But it brought to some of the choicest of our ballads, such as *Sir Patrick Spens*, a fame and vogue such as they had never before enjoyed in the world without ; and it profoundly influenced the poetic thought and taste of Scotland, as of every land where song was loved and English speech was spoken. · One effect was seen in the more strictly Scottish collections of fragments of ballad verse that began soon after to issue from the press.   Herd's, the 'first classical collection of Scottish songs and ballads,' as Scott calls it, appeared in 1769 ; that of Lord Hailes 1770 ; and Pinkerton's in 1781 and 1783. The publication in 1787 of the first volume of Johnson's *Museum* was one of the fruitful results to the national poetry and music of the visit of Robert Burns to Edinburgh ; but the impulse that brought it to the light can be traced back by sure lines to Percy.   Ritson's learned labours in a still wider field came forth between 1780 and 1794 ; and Sibbald's *Chronicle* was of the same year as the *Border Minstrelsy*.

The age of ballad collection and collation had fairly set in.   But this does not deprive the *Minstrelsy* of the praise that, with the beginning of a new century, it ensured that the search for and rescue from oblivion of the old ballads should thenceforth be a business which, not alone the antiquary and the poet, but the whole people should make their concern. Jamieson's *Popular Ballads* followed in 1806; and, after a pause, filled up with the appearance of fresh volumes and fresh editions of the earlier collections, the works of Kinloch, Motherwell, and Buchan came with a rush, in the years 1827-8.

Of these, and other repertories of the national ballads, the number is legion, and the merits and methods as varied and diverse. There is not space to discuss and compare them, even were discussion and comparison part of the present plan. Such treatment is apt to reduce a book on ballads and balladists to what Charles G. Leland terms 'mere logarithmic tables of variants.' First came the harvesters; and then those who were content to glean where the others had left. As matter of course and of necessity the readings, and even the structure of the pieces picked up from oral recitation and singing, presented endless points of difference according to the locality and to the individual singer or collector. As has been said, each old piece of popular poetry, before it has been fixed in print, and even after, takes a certain part of its colour and character from the minds and memories through which it has been strained. As an illustration of this, in another field, one might mention that Pastor Hurt, when he set about, a few years ago, gathering the fragments of Esthonian folk literature, obtained contributions from 633 different collectors, most of them simple peasants, and as the result of three and a half years' work, he brought together 'of epics, lyrics, wedding songs, etc., upwards of 20,000 specimens; of tales about 3000; of proverbs about 18,000; of riddles, about 20,000, besides a large collection of magical formulæ, superstitions, and the like.' These figures include variants of the same tale or ballad theme, of which there were in some cases as many as 160.

The Scottish ballads may scarce be so multitudinous and protean a host as this. But the search for them, and the choice of them when discovered, have given infinite exercise to the industry, the judgment, and the patience of successive editors; and literature has no more curious and romantic chapter than that which deals with ballad collecting and collectors. The latter, in Scotland as elsewhere, have not been free from the human liability to err—few men have been less so. As Percy admitted *Hardyknut* and other examples of the pseudo-antique among his specimens of 'Old Romance Poetry,' Scott's critical acumen did not avail to detect brazen forgeries of Surtees, like *Barthram's Dirge* and *The Death of Featherstonhaugh.* In Cromek's *Relics of Galloway Song* were somewhat palpable 'fakements' of Allan Cunningham; William Motherwell and Peter Buchan made their egregious blunders, and even such careful and experienced antiquaries as Joseph Ritson and David Laing slipped on the dark and broken and intricate paths which they sought to explore. On the whole it can hardly be regretted that our ballad collections bear the impress of the idiosyncrasies of the individual ballad-hunters, as well as of the game they pursued and the district they coursed over.

Scott made his bag, as he tells us, chiefly 'during his early youth,' among 'the shepherds and aged persons in the recesses of the Border mountains,' who 'remembered and repeated the warlike songs of their fathers.' They were gathered on those long pedestrian excursions, with Shortreed or with Leyden (himself a balladist), which were themselves often as full of incident, and of the seeds of future romance, as any old Border raid. The great Master of Romance was, as one of his companions said, 'makin' himsel' a' the time.' Dandie Dinmont, whom the author of *Guy Mannering* sketches from the traits of a dozen honest yeomen and store farmers, whose hospitality he had shared in his rambles through the wilds of Liddesdale, would a few generations earlier have been a stark moss-trooper, ready to ride to the rescue of Kimmont Willie or to seek his 'beef and kail' in the Merse. The raid on Habbie Elliot of the Heughfoot is but a 'variant' of the lifting of Telfer's kye; and *Wandering Willie's Tale*, if it had been cast in verse, would have been the pick of our ballads of 'glamourie,' instead of the choicest of short prose stories. The rhyme and air that haunted the memory of Henry Bertram—what are they but an echo out of Scott's own romantic youth—out of the enchanted land of ballad poetry?

' " Are these the Links of Forth," she said,
   " Or are they the crooks of Dee,
   Or the bonnie woods o' Warroch-head
   That I so fain would see ? " '

It was on one of these excursions up Ettrick that
Scott forgathered with Margaret Laidlaw, the mother of
the 'Shepherd,' and the repository of an inexhaustible
store of fairy tales, songs and ballads, which, as she declared, the compiler of the *Border Minstrelsy* 'spoiled'
by transmitting to print.   But the richest and rarest of
his 'finds' was Hogg himself.   He was nursed in the
lap of the Forest and cradled in ballad and fairy lore.
Here was the 'heart of pathos' of the older poetry; the
head buzzing with its wild fancies; 'the sang o' the
linty amang the broom in the spring'; and along with
these the shaggy front, the strong hand-grips, the loyalty,
and the sturdy sense that are the far-descended inheritance of the Border farmer and shepherd.   Surely, to
parody his own words, those who love to listen to Allan
Ramsay. and Burns and Scott, and to the nameless
Balladists who were their masters and teachers, will
' never forget a'thegither the Ettrick Shepherd.'

More important, however, even than the materials
gathered by Scott from the lips of Mrs. Hogg and other
Border ballad reciters, or from the Glenriddell MSS., was
the golden mine of old poetry, for the preservation of
which he and the nation were indebted to the taste and
retentive memory of Mrs. Brown, daughter of Professor
Thomas Gordon, of King's College, Aberdeen, and

wife of a minister of Falkland, in the beginning of the
century.   There are in existence three MSS. of the songs
and ballads this lady was able to remember as sung
to her on Deeside ; and transcription of her father's
account of this precious collection, as the story is told
by him in a letter to Mr. A. Fraser Tytler, and by him
communicated to Scott, may best and most authentically
explain its origin :—

'An aunt of my children, Mrs. Farquhar, now dead, who
was married to the proprietor of a small estate near the
sources of the Dee, in Braemar, a good old woman who
spent the best part of her life among flocks and herds,
resided in her latter days in the town of Aberdeen.   She
was possessed of a most tenacious memory, which retained
all the songs she had heard from nurses and country-women
in that sequestered part of the country.   Being maternally
fond of my children when young, she had them much about
her, and delighted them with her songs and tales of chivalry.
My youngest daughter, Mrs. Brown, at Falkland, is blessed
with a memory as good as her aunt, and has almost the
whole of her songs by heart.   In conversation, I mentioned
them to your father (William Tytler, the champion of Mary
Stuart) at whose request my grandson, Mr. Scott, wrote
down a parcel of them as her aunt sung them.   Being then
a mere novice in music, he added, in the copy, such musical
notes as, he supposed, would give your father some notion
of the airs, or rather lilts, to which they were sung.'

To all those whose names are mentioned in the
above extract, Scotland and poetry owe a deep debt
of gratitude.   But here again, although men, and men
of learning, have borne their part in the salvage, it is
to the 'spindle side,' and to simple country ears and

memories, that the main acknowledgment is due for saving what it would have been a calamity to lose. What may almost be described as the 'classical text' of some of the finest of our ballads, is that obtained by collation of the Brown 'sets,' of which the fullest is that originally owned by Robert Jamieson, which reappears in revised form in one of the copies possessed by Miss Tytler. From the circumstances of its origin, this text has something of a North Country cast, even where it deals with a South Country theme. But the three divisions of the land, the North, the Centre, and the South, bear a share of the credit of its preservation. The ballads were gathered by Deeside; they were sung and recited under Lomond Law; they were brought before the world by a Borderer.

No such 'finds' are to be looked for any longer. The ground has been for the most part well reaped and gleaned. Only a few ears are to be picked up that have escaped the notice of previous collectors; although, within the last quarter of a century, in quiet corners like the Enzie and Buchan and the Cabrach, the late Dean Christie was still able to gather from the lips of old peasant and fisher women specimens both of ballads and ballad airs that had never been in print. The chief work for half a century has been that of comparing, collating, and critically annotating the materials already found, and reference need only be made to the monumental work in eight volumes of Professor Child, in which the subject of the origins, affinities,

variants and genuine text of both the Scottish and
English ballads has been thoroughly worked out and
brought nearly down to date.

The Ballads themselves have done a greater work.
They have permeated and revived the poetry and
literature of the century like a draught of rare old
wine. The greatest of our modern poets have been
proud to acknowledge what they owe to the forgotten
minstrels who have not sent down to us out of the
darkness, along with their song, so much as their name.
Wordsworth, as well as Scott, pored entranced over
Percy's *Reliques*. Coleridge, Tennyson, Browning,
Swinburne, and a host besides, have drunk delight and
found inspiration in the Scottish ballad minstrelsy; and
it has awakened a responsive chord in the lyre of the
poets of America. As enthusiastic old Christopher
North wrote, 'Perhaps none of us ever wrote verses
of any worth who had not been more or less readers of
our old ballads.'

> 'The Bards are lost,
> The song is saved.'